Puffin Books

The Dwarfs of Nosegay

The dwarfs of Nosegay lived [illegible] t a hundred of them and th[illegible] t-ably on a rabbit's head. [illegible] n they squeezed from the p[illegible] r, but one day a swarm of bees ca[illegible] golden brown cloud and settled on the bra[illegible] pine tree.

'Now we're in trouble,' sai[illegible] old dwarf called Crooked Dirk, for he knew the bees would want to share the honey and there simply wasn't enough for all of them. Not one of the dwarfs knew what to do. They were quite helpless, until little Peter Nosegay, the smallest and youngest dwarf of all, had the idea of knocking at the bees' door and asking for honey, and sure enough they gave him some. 'Little Peter!' cried the other dwarfs, 'you're the bravest dwarf of all our people!' – and as the months went by they realized more and more how much they owed to Peter, for he was a clever dwarf as well as a brave one, and it was his courage and quick thinking that saved them more than once from starving, and kept the friendly rabbits and butterflies safe as well.

These delicately told and simple stories are perfect for reading aloud to very small children, but many older readers too will fall under the spell of this charming miniature world constructed of moorland and sky, heather and dwarfs, bees, rabbits and very little else, yet teeming with busy importance and minutely dramatic events.

Paul Biegel was born in Holland in 1925. He has written more than twenty books for children, many of which have been turned into television series and translated from the original Dutch into other languages. He has won many awards for his books, including the Silver Pencil award for *The Twelve Robbers* and *The Elephant Party*. He is married with two children.

Another book by Paul Biegel

THE ELEPHANT PARTY AND OTHER STORIES

PAUL BIEGEL

The Dwarfs of Nosegay

Translated by Patricia Crampton
Illustrated by Babs van Wely

PUFFIN BOOKS

PUFFIN BOOKS

Published by the Penguin Group
27 Wrights Lane, London W8 5TZ, England
Viking Penguin Inc., 40 West 23rd Street, New York, New York 10010, USA
Penguin Books Australia Ltd, Ringwood, Victoria, Australia
Penguin Books Canada Ltd, 2801 John Street, Markham, Ontario, Canada L3R 1B4
Penguin Books (NZ) Ltd, 182–190 Wairau Road, Auckland 10, New Zealand

Penguin Books Ltd, Registered Offices: Harmondsworth, Middlesex, England

Originally published in the Netherlands as
De Dwergjes van Tuil by Uitgeversmaatschappij
Holland, Haarlem
First published in Great Britain by
Blackie & Son Limited 1978
Published in Puffin Books 1980
10 9 8 7 6 5

Set, printed and bound in Great Britain by
Cox & Wyman Ltd, Reading
Set in Intertype Baskerville

Contents

1 *How the Dwarfs Shared the Honey*

The Dwarfs of Nosegay lived on the moor. There were not two of them, or even half a dozen, but at least a hundred, a whole race of dwarfs.

When the heather flowered they would cry: 'Purple, purple, lovely purple!' and squeeze the honey from the little purple flowers, for the Dwarfs of Nosegay were mad about honey.

But one day a swarm came flying in, a great, golden brown cloud, humming like an engine, and clung humming to the branch of a gnarled pine tree.

'What's that, what's that?' asked Little Peter Nosegay. He was the youngest and always asked everything twice.

'Those are bees, those are bees,' Crooked Dirk Nosegay replied. He answered twice because he liked to tease.

'Now we're in trouble,' said Crooked Dirk.

And they were.

The gnarled pine tree was hollow inside and a hollow tree makes a fine house for bees.

'Zoom!' cried the bees, crawling inside and starting to build cells, cosy little cells made of wax, smooth as a candle. Cells for the children and cells to keep honey in and right in the middle a palace for the queen. Every race of bees has a queen.

When the bee city was finished the trouble began. Now there were two races living on the moor, both of them mad about honey: the Dwarfs of Nosegay and the Bee People of Queen Zoe.

'Go away! Go away! Go away!' shouted the dwarfs next morning. 'The moor belongs to us, the flowers belong to us, the honey belongs to us.'

They shouted at the bees, but there were so many bees, at least a thousand of them, crawling over the purple bells and drawing the honey out of them on their long tongues.

'What are we to do, what are we to do?' cried Little Peter Nosegay. He was afraid of the bees.

'Chase them off,' cried Crooked Dirk. He went ksst! ksst! to the bees but that was no good. He made a spear from a pine needle but the bees simply showed their sharp sting.

With ten other dwarfs of Nosegay, Crooked Dirk shouted to the bees to be gone. But the bees simply went on buzzing and calmly sucking honey out of the little purple flowers.

That evening the dwarfs held a council of war. They

sat down all together in their sandy burrow with the moon for a lamp.

'We must declare war!' shouted Scutch, 'and attack with spears and arrows and swords.'

Scutch was the strongest of the Nosegay Dwarfs.

'Certainly not!' shouted Chick. 'Bees have stings and they are very dangerous. They would sting us to death.'

Chick was the weakest dwarf of Nosegay.

'We mustn't go on yelling like this,' said Tirian. 'We must think. And when I think, I think that what we want is not war but honey. And I think that actually the bees don't want war either, they want honey. We must share the honey.'

Tirian was the best talker of the Dwarfs of Nosegay.

'Share it? How? How?' asked Little Peter. He thought it was a stupid question, but nobody knew the answer. No one knew how.

'I'll think,' said Tirian.

The Dwarfs of Nosegay went to bed, each one under his own clump of heather. The crickets chirped a lullaby and the moon was their night-light.

Little Peter could not sleep; he lay awake thinking. He even took off his cap to think better. How, how, how?

But the sun rose and still Little Peter had not thought of anything and the bees came and Little Peter hid right underneath his clump of heather. He did not even dare to take back his cap because it was hanging neatly on a heather sprig and the heather out there was covered with bees.

'Zoom,' said the bees and that was all they ever said.

They can't talk, thought Little Peter. Perhaps they can't think either.

Not until afternoon when the bees had gone did Little Peter dare to reappear. He picked up his cap.

'Hey!' said Little Peter.

There were purple flowerlets where his cap had hung,

purple flowerlets full of honey, for not a single bee had looked under the cap.

That evening, in the hollow, Little Peter told the others.

Next day there were a hundred dwarfs' caps and a hundred dwarfs' Sunday caps hanging on the heather.

The bees just went on saying zoom and took honey from the sprigs which had no caps.

The Dwarfs of Nosegay shouted hurrah and squeezed the honey from the flowerlets which had been underneath their caps in the evening.

Thanks to Little Peter Nosegay, the youngest.

2 *Little Peter in the Bees' City*

The honey which the dwarfs squeezed out of the purple heather flowers every autumn was for the winter. The dwarfs did not eat it up at once, they stored the honey in pots and only licked their fingers to test it.

But now that the bee people had come to live on the moor, thousands of bees who also took honey from the purple flowers, the dwarfs were not going to have enough full pots for the winter.

'Terrible,' they cried. 'Terrible, what are we to do?'

They *did* have seven potatoes and twelve carrots. These they took every summer from the land Furtherup. They journeyed there with their dwarf cart, dug a fat potato out of the ground, loaded it on the cart and drove back with it. To and fro, to and fro, with one potato or two carrots on each trip. It kept them busy for days.

These were for the winter too, but without honey, the dwarfs were not satisfied.

'I can't get it down my throat,' complained Crooked Dirk. 'It doesn't slip down without honey.'

'It slips down with spit,' said Scutch Nosegay.

They were very careful with the honey but by the middle of the winter the last pot was finished. Completely empty. When you put your tongue into it, all you could find was glass.

'Perhaps there's a flower or two left somewhere on the moor,' thought Little Peter Nosegay. 'One flower . . .'

He put on his fur jacket, took an empty jar and went on a search.

The wind was cold and the heather was as dry as an old broom; it creaked and crackled all round him, but Little Peter Nosegay stepped out bravely.

Just one flower, he kept thinking, but his eyes were running in the wind and he could hardly see anything.

And that was how he suddenly found himself in front of the hollow pine tree. The hollow pine tree, where the Bee People of Queen Zoe lived.

Just a minute, thought Little Peter, the bees will certainly have some honey left. What if I knock and ask for some honey? They couldn't be angry with me for that.

There was no door to be seen; he tried knocking on the trunk, but nothing happened.

Then Little Peter climbed up the rough bark, which went very well, and there, sure enough, he found a hole through which he could climb in.

'Coo-ee!' called Little Peter Nosegay. 'Coo-ee, is there anyone there?'

His voice echoed faintly inside the tree: then there was total silence.

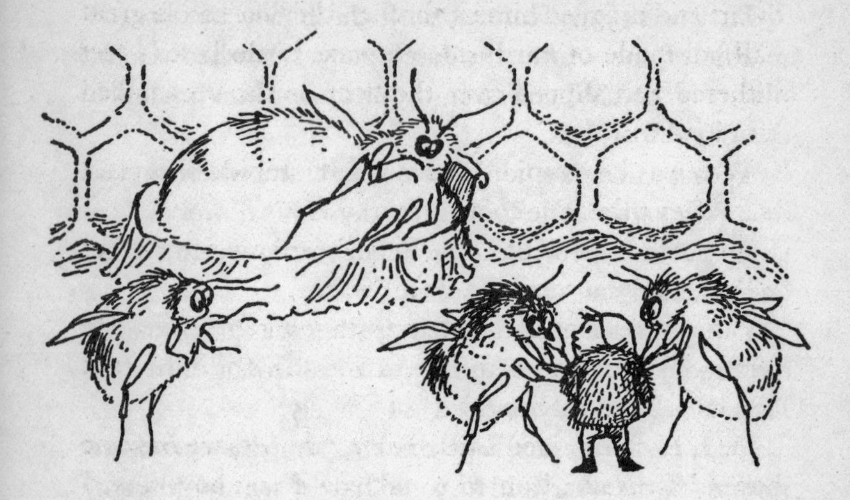

The little dwarf climbed inside and waited until his eyes were used to the darkness.

Then he saw the bee city. Rows and rows of cells, neat and tidy and smooth with wax, like a block of flats with a thousand storeys, and right in the middle a little light was shining.

Perhaps there is someone there, thought Little Peter, sliding downwards. He landed with a plop just in front of the doorway through which the light was shining.

But there were two bees on guard, who darted up and stuck out their sharp stings.

'Zoomm!' they buzzed angrily.

'Oh, help!' said Little Peter. 'Oh, help, I haven't done anything. I just wanted some honey, some honey.'

'Zoomm!' buzzed the bees again. They seized the little dwarf and dragged him in, through the door into a great hall, all made of hard, smooth wax. Little Peter's feet slithered and slipped over the floor as the bees pulled him forward.

Why was I so stupid? he thought, so stupid? Bees can't talk. They think I've come to steal.

But at that moment Little Peter heard a voice saying: 'What have you come for, little dwarf?'

Little Peter looked up. He was standing in a charming room which had a strange smell and straight in front of him lay a huge, fat bee.

'I, I, I,' stammered Little Peter, 'we, we, we have no honey left. And I wanted to ask you if you have any. I mean honey.'

Queen Zoe looked the quaking dwarf over from top to toe. 'I suppose you are the bravest dwarf of your people?' she enquired.

'Oh no, madam, no, no,' said Little Peter.

'Then don't you know how dangerous it is to walk right into a bees' city?' asked Queen Zoe.

'I don't think about it,' said Little Peter, trembling. 'I never think, you see. Almost never.'

'I see! But you did think about honey?' said the queen.

'Yes,' said Little Peter, 'but honey in a flower. I was really looking for a flower.'

The fat queen shook with laughter.

'Flowers in the winter,' she cried. 'You haven't much sense.'

'No, madam,' said Little Peter in a low voice, and bowed his head. He took his cap off, too, and Queen Zoe thought that was very polite.

'Zoomm,' she told the two bees.

Little Peter thought something awful was going to happen, but all the bees did was to take his empty jar, shuffle away with it and come back shortly afterwards with the pot full of honey.

'For a brave, polite dwarf,' said Queen Zoe. 'And when you've finished that, come back for more.'

'Oh,' cried Little Peter, 'thank you, thank you, thank you.' He couldn't stop saying thank you, he was still calling it out on the stairs.

But when he was back in the heather, he shouted to his mates. He showed them the honey and told them the whole story.

'Little Peter,' they cried, 'you're the bravest dwarf of all our people!' And all the Dwarfs of Nosegay danced round him in a ring because they were so pleased about the honey.

3 *The Midwinter Feast*

During the winter the Dwarfs of Nosegay lived under the ground. In the middle of the moor where they lived there was a big mole-hill and when the cold came the dwarfs would creep inside.

Scutch Nosegay went ahead with the lamp, because they had to walk down a dark tunnel, and the other ninety-nine Dwarfs of Nosegay followed. It looked like a wriggly snake of little men, because the tunnel had many bends.

Little Peter Nosegay was the last. He kept on looking round before they went inside the mole-hill. 'Good-bye moor,' he said. 'See you next spring, moor.'

Deep under the ground was a cave which the dwarfs had made into a room. They ate there and they slept there; in the winter they did little else. But just once, they had a feast, the midwinter feast, and the loveliest part of the midwinter feast was the fire.

Little Peter Nosegay was allowed to go with them to collect dry heather twigs. They burned well and did not give off much smoke.

'Put on your fur jacket,' said Tirian Nosegay. 'It's cold outside.'

'And watch out for the crows,' said Chick Nosegay. 'They think you're a mouse, you see, and crows are mad about mice.'

Old Crooked Dirk Nosegay went too; he could carry even the biggest pieces of firewood.

It had been snowing on the moor; there were white patches everywhere, where the wind had swept the snow into drifts.

'All go in different directions,' said Tirian, 'but don't go too far.'

Little Peter went to the left.

'Dry twigs, dry twigs, dry twigs,' he kept repeating to himself. He looked under every clump of heather and even under the snowdrifts, but it was very cold there. His hands were turning bright red.

Now and then Little Peter looked up to make sure there were no black crows flying overhead. He could not see anything, but after a while he heard cawing in the distance and three of the black jackanapes bore down on him with beating wings

Help, thought Little Peter, what shall I do?

Crows fly fast; they have sharp eyes and Little Peter had no time to run back to the mole-hill.

I must hide, he thought, and he dived straight into a snowdrift. He dug his way right into it until even his feet were out of sight.

Cold, cold, cold, shuddered Little Peter. But better cold, he thought, than caught by a crow.

He dug his way still deeper into the snow and there he felt something strange, something hairy, something thready, not a twig, but perhaps it would burn well. Little Peter waited for a long time until he was quite stiff with cold, then he turned himself round and stared out. Not a crow to be seen, not a caw to be heard. He pulled the thready thing out of the snow and ran back with it to the mole-hill.

'What have you got there?' asked Chick Nosegay, 'an animal?'

'No,' said Little Peter, 'not an animal.'

'Something belonging to humans, I expect,' said Tirian Nosegay. 'Couldn't you find anything better? I'm sure that funny thing won't burn.'

'I was afraid of the crows,' said Little Peter.

'So were we,' said Crooked Dirk, 'but we collected firewood, all the same.' Crooked Dirk had a big bundle of dry twigs on his back.

They went inside with their twigs and Little Peter followed them with his funny thing. Perhaps it will burn, after all, he thought.

The fire was built in the middle of the room. The twigs of heather crackled cheerily and the flames made dancing dwarf shadows on the wall. It was a fine mid-winter feast, with scraps of roast potato, baked chunks of orange carrot and honey, honey, honey. They ate up the whole pot which the Queen Bee had given them.

Then Little Peter picked up his funny thready thing to throw on the fire, but he had to pause when the smoke made him cough.

'Hey! Stop!' cried Ianto Nosegay. Ianto was the eldest dwarf of the Dwarfs of Nosegay. 'You mustn't burn that,' he said, 'that's a chrysalis.'

'What?' asked Little Peter, 'what did you say, Old Ianto?'

'That's a chrysalis,' said Ianto. 'A butterfly will come out of that in the spring.'

'Oh,' said Little Peter. 'I didn't know that. I picked it up instead of firewood.'

'It will be all bright and beautiful,' said Ianto. 'Take good care of it. After the winter you must hang the chrysalis on your clump of heather so that you can see the butterfly coming out for yourself.'

'Beautiful, beautiful!' cried all the dwarfs, except Chick and Crooked Dirk. They did not dare to say anything.

But Tirian Nosegay did. 'Yes,' he said, 'I can see it too now. When we were outside there was too much snow on it.'

Tirian Nosegay was a good talker.

When the dwarfs went to sleep after their feast – they always slept until March – Little Peter dreamed of his butterfly. It was a butterfly with red wings, like two red flames, just as if he had actually found something to put on the fire.

4 *Little Peter Stays at Home*

The Dwarfs of Nosegay lifted their faces to the spring sunshine. They had slept through most of the winter, deep underground in their cave, but now it was April; the heather was beginning to turn green and the sun was bright gold.

'Where's Little Peter?' asked Dirk Nosegay.

'He's dreaming again,' said Tirian.

The dwarfs began to laugh.

'Ask him to go and fetch some honey,' said Tirian. 'He can get it from Queen Zoë in the Bee City in the hollow tree.'

'Why don't you go yourself?' asked Crooked Dirk.

'Oh,' said Tirian, 'I think fetching honey is a job for our youngest. And for the time being that is Peter.'

Tirian was a good talker but he didn't dare to go. None of the Dwarfs of Nosegay dared to go to the Bee

City except for Little Peter. He had already been there once or twice and brought back a full pot of honey with him.

Crooked Dirk stood up, stretched to his full height (but he was still crooked) and went to have a look at the clump of heather where Little Peter lived.

'What are you doing?' he asked. 'Just sitting dreaming?'

'I'm sitting watching,' said Little Peter. 'I'm sitting watching my chrysalis.'

'What's that you say?' asked Crooked Dirk.

'My chrysalis,' said Little Peter. 'There, that's my chrysalis.' He pointed to the thready thing, which was hanging by one thread from the heather. 'A butterfly is coming out of that,' he said, 'a beautiful butterfly.'

Dirk suddenly remembered that Little Peter had found the chrysalis when they were looking for firewood for the midwinter feast.

'I can't see anything coming,' said Crooked Dick.

'It moved a little,' said Little Peter. 'This morning it moved a little.'

'That's sure to have been the wind,' said Crooked Dirk. 'I think it will be a long time yet. Couldn't you go and get some honey?'

Little Peter shook his head. 'I must stay and watch,' he said. 'I want to see my butterfly coming out, my butterfly.'

Crooked Dirk went back to the other dwarfs.

'He won't do it,' he said.

Then all the Dwarfs of Nosegay went to Little Peter's

heather clump and said, 'We'll look after your chrysalis if you will fetch the honey.'

But Little Peter shook his head.

'I want to see my own butterfly coming out,' he said, 'My own butterfly.'

Three days later nothing had happened. The chrysalis was hanging completely still from its heather twig and after six days it was still hanging there.

'You could have gone and fetched the honey six times over,' said the dwarfs. 'It wasn't nice of you.'

But Little Peter just shook his head.

On the seventh day the chrysalis moved again. It shook and quivered; there was no wind.

Little Peter jumped to his feet and watched open-mouthed, because a miracle was taking place. The threaded shape broke open and something wet and sticky crawled out. It did not look in the least like a butterfly, it looked like a broken umbrella, but little by little the umbrella grew bigger and stronger and less crumpled and suddenly Little Peter saw the wings. Two great wings, red, white and black.

'Butterfly!' he cried. 'Hello, butterfly, I'm Little Peter!'

But the butterfly continued to hang quite still, upside down, with her wings underneath.

Little Peter crept a little closer and began to stroke the wings with a cautious fingertip.

The creature trembled.

'Don't be frightened,' whispered Little Peter. 'Please

don't be frightened. I won't hurt you. I like you very much, you're beautiful, beautiful.'

Suddenly he thought of a name for his butterfly: Daphne.

'Hello, Daphne,' said Little Peter. 'You're called Daphne because that's a beautiful name. And you must stay with me and we'll be friends.'

But the butterfly was quivering more and more strongly and she began to creep backwards towards the end of the twig.

'Don't go!' cried Little Peter. 'Don't go away, you mustn't.'

But the butterfly turned round, poised right side up on the tip of the twig and began to beat her wings.

'Daphne,' cried Little Peter. 'Hey, Daphne, stop, Daphne!'

He stood right in front of her, spreading out his little arms to hold her back. 'I'll get honey for you, honey. And everything you want, everything.'

But it looked as if the butterfly had not even seen the little dwarf. She turned her feelers in all directions and suddenly she fluttered away, like a leaf in the wind.

'Daphne!' Little Peter shouted. 'Daphne, stay here!'

But the butterfly rose higher and higher into the blue sky until she seemed to vanish in the golden sun. There were tears in Little Peter's eyes, he could see nothing for a moment, but when he looked up Crooked Dirk was standing in front of him.

'What's up with you?' asked Crooked Dick. 'Why are you crying?'

'Oh, nothing,' said Little Peter.

'Are you crying about your butterfly?' asked Crooked Dirk.

'Oh, nothing,' said Little Peter again.

But Crooked Dirk had seen it all. 'You know,' he said, 'butterflies have to fly, you can't keep them.'

'She was so beautiful,' said Little Peter, 'and sweet.'

'She'll be coming back,' said Crooked Dirk. 'She'll come by from time to time. But if you try to keep her she'll die of grief.'

Little Peter didn't answer, but he understood.

'So will you go and get the honey now?' asked Crooked Dirk.

'All right,' said Little Peter. He didn't feel so sad now, because he knew that he would see Daphne again.

5 *The Meadow*

The Dwarfs of Nosegay had sent Little Peter Nosegay to the bees in the hollow tree city to fetch honey.

Little Peter knew the way because he had been there several times. This time, too, he climbed bravely up the tree trunk with his empty jar, crawled in through the hole and let himself slide down inside the tree, past the wax cells, row on row, at least a thousand of them, down to the bottom where the entrance to Queen Zoe's palace lay.

'How busy everyone is,' thought Little Peter.

There was a great buzzing and scrabbling all round him, as if he had arrived in a human city filled with traffic.

Is there something going on? thought Little Peter. Before, it had always been very still and silent, with just two guards at the door.

They were there still. They bowed to the dwarf and let

him pass, but even in Queen Zoe's palace everyone was busy. The passages and rooms were teeming with bees. They rushed up to Little Peter and sniffed him and tickled his face with their feelers.

'Don't you do anything to me!' cried Little Peter anxiously. 'The Queen knows me, you know! She knows me very well!'

Zoom went the bees, and nothing more.

Little Peter walked on, but he was constantly bumping into other bees who sniffed him and by the time he was standing by Queen Zoe at last he was panting violently.

'What's the matter, my dwarf?' asked Queen Zoe. She lay stretched out in her lovely room and she was very large and very stout.

'Everyone's so very busy,' said Little Peter. 'And there are so many bees about.'

'It's spring, my dwarf,' said Queen Zoe. 'You've only been here in the winter when all the bees are asleep except for me,' said Queen Zoe, yawning loudly. 'But in the spring my people wake up and begin to fly out again to collect more honey.'

'Oh,' said Little Peter. 'Honey, yes, that's what I really came for. Have you a little left for us? Honey?' He held up his little empty jar.

Before, Queen Zoe had always nodded kindly and ordered the pot to be filled with honey. But now she lifted herself half upright and stared at the dwarf with strange eyes.

'No, my dwarf,' she said. 'I don't give away honey in the spring. You can go and find it for yourself.'

'But-but-but,' stuttered Little Peter, 'the heather isn't in flower yet. The heather, the heather doesn't flower until autumn.'

Queen Zoe fell back again.

'Silly dwarf,' she said, 'you must look in other flowers, buttercups and dandelions and clover. They are in flower. Off you go.'

'Oh. Oh yes,' said Little Peter. 'Thank you.'

'It's a good thing,' said the Queen, 'that you say thank you. Let the other dwarfs of Nosegay do the same thing one day. There would be no harm in their bringing me a present, for all the honey.'

Little Peter blushed right round to his ears. 'Oh, oh

yes,' he stammered. 'I'll tell them, a little present.'

Little Peter was still red when he was standing outside the hollow tree. How are we to do it? he thought. How are we to do it? Where can I find buttercups and dandelions and clover?

He wandered over the wide moor where nothing was in flower yet, but suddenly he saw something moving. Something was fluttering close to the ground and it was coming nearer and nearer.

'Daphne!' shouted Little Peter suddenly. 'Daphne!'

It was his butterfly, the butterfly he had watched coming out of her chrysalis.

Little Peter stood stock still; perhaps that would make her come closer. But then the little dwarf held his breath, because the butterfly had landed on his shoulder.

'Daphne,' he murmured softly. 'Dear Daphne, how sweet you are.'

She smelled good. She smelled of honey.

'Daphne,' whispered Little Peter. 'Where did you get it from? The honey?'

The butterfly moved her feelers and flew into the air. Little Peter began to run after her. I'm mad, he thought, she didn't understand me at all. But still, he went on running and it actually looked as if the butterfly was glancing back to see where he was.

Little Peter's heart began to thump. Louder and faster it went. He was getting tired and he was scratched by the hard twigs of heather. I can't keep up, he thought, I can't keep up any more.

But Daphne flew on and the little dwarf went on running after her.

Then suddenly, Little Peter came to a hedge. The butterfly flew over it and Little Peter cried: 'Hold on!' because he had to wriggle between the tough twigs of the hedge and he was so tired, so very tired.

But at last he appeared, panting, on the other side.

'Oooh!' cried Little Peter.

Before him lay a meadow. It looked like a sea, not of water, but of flowers: yellow and red and white. Dandelions, buttercups and clover.

'Thank you!' he shouted towards the blue sky. 'Thank you, dear Daphne!'

He picked a big bunch, as much as he could carry, and ran back with it to his mates, the hundred Dwarfs of Nosegay on the moor.

Now they had honey in the spring as well. They could fetch as much as they wanted from the meadow. And as you know, the Dwarfs of Nosegay are mad about honey.

6 *Visit to the Bees*

For three days the Dwarfs of Nosegay enjoyed themselves in their newly-found meadow. They rolled among the grasses, they lay in the sun and they sucked honey from the flowers. There was more than enough for bees and dwarfs at once.

'And we have Daphne to thank for it,' Little Peter kept repeating.

'Yes,' said Ianto the Eldest, 'Yes, but we have to thank Queen Zoe too.'

'Oh,' cried Little Peter in horror. 'Oh yes, Ianto, I had nearly forgotten. We must take Queen Zoe a present to say thank you to her.'

'Of course,' said Ianto. 'For all the honey she gave us for the winter. I have been thinking about it. But what?'

The dwarfs began to think.

'Something gold,' cried Crooked Dirk. 'A queen must have gold.'

'But we haven't any gold, have we?' asked Chick Nosegay.

'Yes, we have,' cried Scutch. 'We have some golden paper. It shines beautifully.'

Scutch Nosegay was shining himself with pride. He was the strongest and bravest dwarf, who had found the thin cardboard packet. It had come from human beings and the letters CIGARETTES were written on it, but inside there was gold paper. The dwarfs had hoarded it carefully.

'Now, what can the Queen do with it?' asked Tirian Nosegay. He was a very good thinker.

Ianto Nosegay said nothing. Ianto was the eldest and he went on staring into the fire. All the dwarfs were sitting round it that evening in the big hollow in the middle of the moor. 'A crown,' said Ianto suddenly. 'We'll make a crown out of gold paper. That will be just right for a bee.'

Work began the next day. With scissors and knives,

very small, fine work, full of decorative points and circles. It turned into a brilliant bee crown with an opening at the top to allow Queen Zoe's feelers to stick out. They packed it carefully in a basket made of heather twigs and then the hundred Dwarfs of Nosegay made their way to the bees' hollow tree.

It was quite a job getting the basket up the tree to the entrance to Bee City. Little Peter crawled in first, to tell the bees to expect a visit.

After a little while he came back. 'Queen Zoe will receive us on the square before her palace,' he said. 'But not more than five of us. Five, she said, otherwise it will be too crowded.'

Ianto the Eldest went along, with Crooked Dirk and Tirian, but Chick was quaking with fear. All those sharp stings, he thought. 'You go,' he told Jung Nosegay, who was never allowed to do anything. But this time he was.

Little Peter showed the way. Cautiously they climbed down inside the hollow tree; there were plenty of knobs for their hands and feet. And suddenly the party lights went on.

'How glorious,' cried Crooked Dirk.

'Wax candles,' said Tirian.

There lay the Bee City, in a golden glow of tiny flames. Houses and more houses with at least a thousand cells one above the other, narrow streets and a broad square where a fantastic palace stood, all made of shining bees' wax.

Queen Zoe came out, but not on her own feet. She was drawn along on her couch, by six guard bees.

The dwarfs politely removed their caps and Little Peter stepped forward. 'We have come to thank you,' he said. 'For the honey. And we have a present, a present for you.'

'Ah!' said the Queen, 'and who are these gentlemen?'

'Oh,' cried Little Peter, shocked. 'Oh, pardon your Majesty. This is Ianto, Ianto the Eldest, and Dirk, Crooked Dirk, and Tirian and Chick – no! – Jung.'

'How do you do, Chick-No-Jung,' said the Queen kindly. 'What a beautiful name you have!'

Nobody dared to say anything about this mistake, but Ianto quickly opened the basket and took out the golden crown.

'Mmmm!' buzzed the Queen and a thousand bees in the square all buzzed together, 'Mmmy mmy!' The sound was deafening and rather scarey, but Queen Zoe set the shining crown on her head and it fitted exactly. Her imposing feelers poked elegantly through the top.

'Thank you, Dwarfs of Nosegay,' she said. 'I shall wear this crown every Sunday. And during the week I shall keep it in the basket.'

Then the bees began to dance. The dwarfs had never seen this happening and, in fact, the bee dance is a rare sight. On their six legs, with quivering wings and swaying feelers, they tripped past each other and over each other, forming the strangest patterns. Like clouds, changing from a dragon into a ship, and then into a leaping dog, but much, much quicker.

The dwarfs looked on open-mouthed and the bees immediately pushed honey into them, for this was a party.

'Now you,' said Queen Zoe, and the dwarfs sang their ditty as they had agreed beforehand.

We are the dwarfs of the moor
And Nosegay is our name.
We live with the bees on the moor
And we're very glad they came.

High up on the branch of the hollow tree sat the other ninety-five dwarfs all in a row, singing pom-pom, pom-pom down through the hole to keep time.

They ate some more honey and then Little Peter, Ianto, Tirian, Crooked Dirk and Chick-No-Jung climbed out again with round tummies.

'Was it nice? Was it nice?' cried ninety-five little voices.

But how could they tell?

7 *Daphne Gets Married*

Little Peter and Crooked Dirk were on their way to the meadow with empty jars. The meadow was beyond the hedge at the end of the moor, where the Dwarfs of Nosegay lived.

'There's lots,' said Little Peter. 'Lots of honey this spring.'

'Yes, lots,' said Crooked Dirk. 'Lots-lots. You say everything double.'

They crawled through the hedge. The meadow was blue with blossom – and white, and yellow. There were dandelions, buttercups, clover, cowslips and forget-me-nots.

'You take the cups,' said Crooked Dirk, 'and I'll take the lips.'

Little Peter laughed, like a mouse squeaking. 'I'll take the clover,' he cried. 'There's much more in the clover. You take the red ones, I'll take the white.'

They went to work, squeezing, squeezing all the honey

from the flowers, but sometimes it was: 'Oh, sorry, Mr Bee,' because there was a busy bee on the clover and he must not be disturbed. That was the agreement.

Suddenly Little Peter looked up. 'Daphne!' he cried. 'Daphne!'

A big butterfly, coloured red and white and black, was fluttering overhead, like a leaf from a tree. She heard Little Peter's voice and settled on his shoulder. She was very big, but not at all heavy.

'You're tickling!' cried Little Peter.

Daphne knew Little Peter well. The dwarf had found her when she was still a caterpillar in a chrysalis, he had seen her come out and become a butterfly, he had given her the name Daphne and Daphne had shown him the way to the meadow of flowers.

'You're still tickling!' cried Little Peter. You're tick –'

But before he could say it twice his mouth fell open with surprise. For the second tickle came from a second butterfly, also red and white and black, which was sitting on his other shoulder.

'Is this your friend, Daphne? Have you got a friend?'

cried Little Peter. And he shouted to Crooked Dirk: 'Look here!'

Crooked Dirk set down his honey pot.

'Those two are going to be married. You can see that,' he said wisely.

'Oh,' said Little Peter. 'Oh Daphne, if you're getting married you'll have children. How many children?'

'Of course not, dummy,' said Crooked Dirk. 'Not butterflies. They lay eggs which turn into caterpillars and they – '

'Yes yes,' said Little Peter. 'Of course. I knew that. Poor Daphne. You'll never see your own children. But I'll look after them for you, you know, your children.'

'What a job,' said Crooked Dirk. 'Is your pot full yet?'

But Little Peter was looking at the other butterfly. 'He's very fine, your fiancé,' he said. 'Fine. He's called Jacob. I thought of that. Jacob.'

'They'll be getting married tomorrow morning,' said Crooked Dirk. 'Butterflies always get married early in the morning.'

That evening, round the fire in the big hollow, Little Peter began to talk about the wedding. 'We must go and celebrate,' he said.

Ianto, the eldest of the Dwarfs of Nosegay, thought that was a good idea. 'How many of us would you like to go, Little Peter?' he asked.

'All hundred of us,' cried Little Peter. 'All of us, and each with a flower in his cap.'

Even before the sun was above the ground, a long line

of a hundred dwarfs was curling over the moor like a snake. The snake crawled through the hedge to the middle of the meadow and there it broke in two. One half, fifty dwarfs, formed the letter D for Daphne, the other fifty the letter J for Jacob. And each one stuck a great dandelion in his cap to make the letters look as if they were made of gold.

Just then the first rays of the sun fell on them; there was a blaze of colour and at the same moment the bride and bridegroom came flying up. But not alone. A great, whirling cloud of butterflies in many bright colours was hovering behind them.

'Hurrah!' cried Little Peter. 'Hurrah!'

But Crooked Dirk began to laugh. 'Look here,' he said, 'those butterflies can't even read!' For Jacob had settled in front of the D and Daphne in front of the J.

'Other way round, other way round!' cried Little Peter.

But the bridal pair did not understand. 'Other way round, other way round' must of course be the solemn words of the marriage ceremony, thought Jacob, and he embraced Daphne tenderly.

'Not yet, not yet!' cried Little Peter.

But Daphne thought, I'm married now! And she embraced Jacob tenderly back again.

Ianto laid his hand on Little Peter's shoulder. 'It's all right like this,' he said. 'The butterflies are very happy, even if they can neither read nor speak.'

'Oh,' said Little Peter. 'Oh, but? I mean, what about our song?'

'Of course,' said Ianto.

And there in the middle of the meadow in the early morning, the Dwarfs of Nosegay sang the three-part wedding song of Jacob and Daphne, while all the butterflies fluttered round and round their heads and the bees from the hollow tree hummed deep organ notes.

It was even nicer than in church.

Come, sing, you dwarfs from far and wide,
Your song for Daphne, flying bride.
Dwarfs, come beat the booming drum
For Jacob Butterfly, the groom.

Afterwards the bridal pair flew steadily up towards the blue sky, higher and higher. The dwarfs put their heads right back to watch the butterflies and ninety-nine caps fell on the grass. One didn't, and that was Little Peter's, because he was waving it.

'I'll look after your children, Daphne!' he called after her.

And he kept his word.

8 *Wire Netting*

On the other side of the moor lay the land of Furtherup. Potatoes and carrots and lettuce grew there and in the summer the Dwarfs of Nosegay always went to see if the potatoes were fat enough and the carrots long enough and orange enough. Then the dwarfs would dig one or two out of the ground and take them back for the winter. They used their little cart, dragging the potatoes one by one and the carrots two at a time, bumpety-bump over the moor, pushing and panting and sweating. Pooff, it was hard work!

'Come on,' said Ianto the Eldest one day. 'Let's go and have a look.'

The summer sun was beginning to sink.

Little Peter, Crooked Dirk and Scutch Nosegay went with him.

It was a long way to walk; the path wriggled through the tall heather, making at least fifty bends. On the last bend Little Peter cried: 'Have a look! Look there!'

In the land Furtherup stood four fat elephants. They were pushing and shoving as if they couldn't get through, couldn't cross the border. Elephants – well – they were rabbits, but to the dwarfs they seemed like elephants, they were so big.

'Hi there, Eartwitcher,' cried Ianto. 'What's going on?' He knew the rabbits well. They liked carrots, too, and lettuce, in particular.

'Wire,' cried Eartwitcher.

Little Peter had seen it already. He was not at all afraid of the elephant-size rabbits and had gone racing up to them.

'A fence!' he cried. 'A high wire fence.'

'And strong, too,' said the rabbit. 'We've been pushing at it for an hour already, and we're hungry.'

'Hm,' said Ianto. 'Small holes. Could you get through, Little Peter?'

'My head could,' said the little dwarf. 'My head.' He looked like a fish in a net, standing there with his head poked through the wire. 'But not the rest of me – ouch, my ears!'

'Silly,' said Scutch Nosegay. 'You'll have to climb over it. That's all.'

He began at once, because Scutch was the bravest and strongest of them. 'Like a rope-ladder,' he cried. 'Nothing to it.'

But the wire fence was very high indeed.

'Where is he now?' asked Tibby. Tibby had weak, rabbit's eyes; his world was fuzzy. 'Stick to looking with your nose,' was what Eartwitcher always told him, because Tibby could smell very well.

'Be careful now, Scutch!' cried Ianto.

Scutch was a mere dot, high in the air.

'I can see right across the moor!' Scutch called down to them. 'Lovely view – oh, there's someone coming. A human being. A man.'

This was the farmer who grew the potatoes and carrots and lettuce in the land Furtherup. He ate them too, and so did his wife and children. That was why he had put up the wire fence, to stop the rabbits. The farmer knew nothing about the Dwarfs of Nosegay.

'Oh help, Scutch! Come down!' shouted Ianto.

But Scutch was already over the top of the fence. He had no time to climb back again. He did climb down, and quickly, but on the other side of the fence, into the land of Furtherup.

'Hide, Scutch!' cried Little Peter anxiously. 'Hide, quickly!'

They could already hear the farmer's footsteps, swish-swish through the tall heather.

Scutch crept under a potato plant. Eartwitcher, Tibby and the other rabbits found hiding places among the little fir trees, with the dwarfs between them.

'Oh help,' cried Little Peter. 'Oh help, I hope it's all right. All the – '

'Psst!' hissed Ianto.

The farmer was inside the fence. He too had come to see whether the potatoes were fat enough and the carrots long enough and to pick some lettuces, because they had grown big enough to be eaten.

'What if he starts weeding?' began Little Peter, trembling.

'Psst!' hissed Ianto.

They stared through the fir trees.

The farmer strolled over the land Furtherup. Five minutes, ten minutes, an hour. But he didn't weed, he only looked, once quite close to the potato plant where Scutch was hiding.

Ianto put his hand over Little Peter's mouth, because he had nearly screamed.

'Scutch isn't afraid,' whispered Ianto.

Then the farmer pulled up twelve lettuces, dropped them in a bag, went out through the door in the fence and locked it, before walking across the moor. Swish-swish, until there was no more sound to be heard.

'Scutch!' called Ianto. 'Are you still there?'

'No!' called Scutch. 'I'm here.'

He was already among the carrots.

'They're not orange enough yet,' he called, 'and the potatoes are too small.'

Scutch really was brave. He climbed back over the fence, almost as high as the blue sky, and jumped to the ground.

'They'll be ripe next week,' he said. 'Then we can bring the cart.'

'Yes, yes,' said Ianto. 'But how are we to get the potatoes and carrots through the fence?'

That was the question – for the dwarfs and for the rabbits.

'Tirian will have to work something out,' said Scutch. 'He's the best thinker in Nosegay.'

But Little Peter was another one.

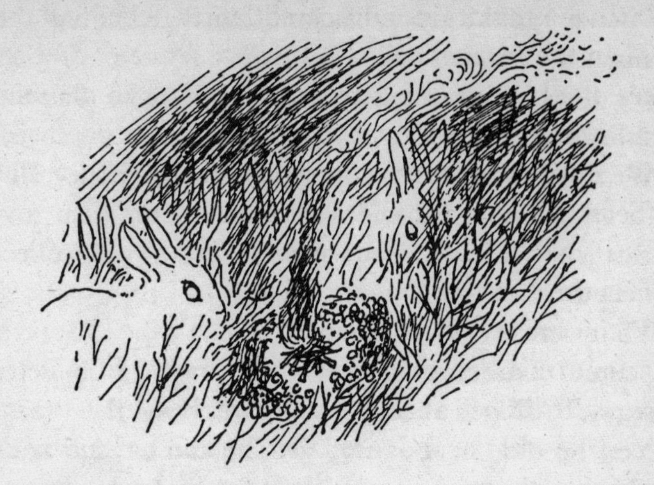

9 *Up, Up and Away*

'But couldn't you dig?' cried Tirian Nosegay. 'Just go straight underneath?'

The dwarfs were sitting in their dell in the middle of the big moor and their brushwood fire was crackling merrily. The moon was out and the starry sky gave only a faint light but the flames shone red on the dwarfs' cheeks; they shone on the rabbits' noses too, because there were twelve rabbits sitting in a ring round the edge of the dell. This was called the Great Assembly.

They were talking about the land Furtherup, which had a wire fence round it, with such small holes that no one could get through it. Nor could any of the potatoes or carrots or lettuce which grew there, behind the wire.

'No,' said Eartwitcher. 'We have dug, but the wire

goes down into the ground as well.' Eartwitcher had the strongest rabbit paws.

'We shall die of hunger,' said Tibby, who was the fattest rabbit.

'We shan't,' said Ianto Nosegay. 'We have honey. But we need potatoes for the winter, seven at least, and carrots – about thirty-three of them. We always collect them in the cart.'

What were they to do now?

'Scutch climbed over the wire,' cried Little Peter Nosegay. 'Climbed all the way. He was brave!'

'Yes, he did,' said Ianto. 'But he can't climb back again with a heavy potato or carrot on his back.'

'No,' said Tirian Nosegay. 'He will have to saw them up and split the pieces into smaller pieces. Small pieces of carrot and potato will go through the wire.'

Not a bad idea of Tirian's.

But Ianto said: 'That's too hard work for one dwarf; even sawing and splitting all day, you could only deal with two carrots.'

The rabbits laughed grimly. Two carrots was only half a dish for half a rabbit.

Little Peter looked up at the stars. Some of them winked back at him and suddenly he had the answer. 'Ianto,' he said, 'if all of us, the whole hundred, went to the land Furtherup with saws and axes, could we make the pieces, and pieces of pieces?'

'Yes, my boy, but no one dares to climb like me,' said Scutch.

'We could fly,' said Little Peter. 'Fly through the air.'

That Peter! All the hundred dwarfs round the fire began to laugh and all the rabbits round the dell: Hee hee hee, ha ha ha!

But Little Peter did not blush with shame. He had a plan.

Next morning Little Peter went to the hollow pine tree. He climbed up, crawled in through the hole, dropped down to the Bee City and knocked politely on the door of Queen Zoe's palace.

An hour later Little Peter was back. All hundred dwarfs ran out and gazed open-mouthed at the air above Little Peter. For there hovered a dark cloud, rumbling like thunder. Bees. Hundreds of bees.

'The cart!' cried Little Peter, 'and the saws and axes. And the big basket. The cart, quickly.'

'Have you gone crazy?' asked Crooked Dirk.

'We're going flying,' said Little Peter. 'Flying!'

'Psha!' went the dwarfs.

But Ianto said: 'The cart, the saws, the axes. Hup!'

There went the Dwarfs of Nosegay, all hundred of them across the moor, like a long wriggly snake to the land Furtherup. Bonkety-bonk went the cart, scritch-scratch sang the saws and axes in the basket, and the dark cloud rumbled above their heads.

Little Peter had brought along a lot of grass rope. At the wire fence he tied the rope to the basket – at least twenty pieces of it – and the bees began to pull, with their feet, with their jaws, and with wings beating twice as hard as usual.

Up went the basket.

'Hey!' shouted Ianto.

'Hurrah!' cried Little Peter. 'In a minute we'll sit in it ourselves and fly. Fly, one by one, in the basket.'

The dwarfs turned pale.

'I'm going to climb,' said Scutch. He had already started, like the first time.

But Little Peter cried: 'Who's going to be first!'

The basket was already coming down empty.

Brave Little Peter. He was the first Dwarf of Nosegay

to take a flying trip, high, high up in the basket and he was scared, scared, scared. But suddenly he saw someone who was fluttering even higher in the air. Daphne, and Jacob too. Two happily married butterflies.

'Daphne!' screamed Little Peter. 'Daphne, I'm flying! Where are your children? Where, Daphne?'

She made no answer but flew towards the willow trees on the other side of the land Furtherup.

There? thought Little Peter. But the basket thudded to the ground and he had to jump out quickly.

That morning the land was teeming with dwarfs. One group was busy digging up carrots, another group potatoes. Others were shoving and rolling them towards the fence, where there were at least twelve waiting to saw and split. The carrots were sawn in discs and the discs chopped into splinters with the axe. The splinters were pushed through the wire and loaded on the cart.

But the potatoes were so thick that it was impossible to saw through them. There wasn't a hope.

'We'll have to stick to carrots,' Ianto decided, and the potato diggers started pulling up lettuce leaves, tearing them in strips and putting them through the wire for twelve rabbits who were standing on the other side with quivering noses.

'Thank you, thank you,' cried Eartwitcher, but Tibby went on calling: 'More, more,' with his mouth full.

'Stop!' called Ianto as the sun went down, for the farmer usually came to look at his land in the late afternoon.

First the saws and axes were flown back and then the dwarfs, one by one in the basket, high in the air, shivering, shaking and quaking.

'Thank you, bees!' they called. 'Thank you very much!'

The cloud flew off humming, *whoosh* to the hollow tree.

The dwarfs took longer about it, with their fully-laden cart.

'Thank you,' said the rabbits, but they were worried. Surely this couldn't be done every day?

Ianto was worried too. Chopped up carrots don't keep very well and they had no potatoes at all. Would Little Peter be able to think of something better?

10 *Little Peter Finds a Boat*

Little Peter Nosegay was walking all alone across the big moor, trying to think – about the wire fence round the land Furtherup, about the potatoes which would not go through it, about Daphne and Jacob who were going to have caterpillar children, but where?

'I can't think about it all,' Little Peter whispered to himself. 'I can't think properly. Tirian can do it better.'

But Tirian Nosegay had been gruff that morning and Crooked Dirk had only laughed, so Little Peter had gone away.

Round a bend in the path he met Tibby, sniffing the air with his rabbit nose. 'Where are you off to?' asked Tibby.

'Somewhere,' said Little Peter. 'Can you smell something?'

'No,' said Tibby. 'Sand and heather, nothing else.'

'Can you hear them too?' asked Little Peter. 'Can you

hear sand and heather? Your ears are so big that I could get right inside them. Right inside, standing up straight.'

'Oh yes,' said Tibby, 'but what I can hear now is an inquisitive dwarf asking funny questions.'

'Oh,' said Little Peter. 'Can I get on your back?'

'Where do you want to go?' asked Tibby.

'To Furtherup,' said Little Peter.

'What do you want there?'

'To look. Just to have a look.'

'Through the wire?'

'Yes,' said Little Peter. 'Through the wire. Perhaps there's a twig we could use to pull a lettuce leaf towards us. A lettuce leaf.'

Tibby crouched close to the ground so that Little Peter could climb on his back. 'Hang on tightly to my ears,' he said and set off at a gallop for Furtherup.

'Perhaps there is a hole somewhere, after all. A hole I can get through,' said Little Peter.

Tibby ran the full length of the fence, Little Peter steering by his ears and shouting from time to time: 'Wait a moment, slower, slower, stand still,' while he gripped the rabbit's fur with his little legs. But the fence was new and strong; no little holes had opened or rusted through anywhere.

They ran to the very end, and there was a ditch. 'Hallo,' said Little Peter, 'water! I didn't know that. Water, here?'

'Can you swim?' asked Tibby.

But moorland dwarfs can't swim. They prefer dry land.

'Look,' said Tibby. 'Someone has left a clog here.' He sniffed at an old clog lying in the tall grass. 'Yes, yes, poof, it's the farmer's.'

But Little Peter did not say 'poof'. Little Peter said: 'A boat.' He said it just once: a boat.

'What do you mean?' asked Tibby.

Then Little Peter burst out: 'A boat, a boat, a boat. We can go in that, down the ditch, round the fence, to Furtherup. And there, and back, and there, and back, with a potato every time. Push it into the ditch, Tibby. A potato every time. A fat one. Push!'

Little Peter's words were tumbling over each other. He was thinking so fast, he was thinking better than Tirian Nosegay.

And Tibby pushed with his nose and Little Peter shoved with his little arms, one two, hup!

The clog surged like a great cargo boat on to the water.

'It would take two potatoes at once!' cried Little Peter.

'Better get some lettuce,' said Tibby. 'I don't eat potatoes.'

They couldn't find a stick. How was Little Peter to row the boat? But there were reeds growing further down and Tibby gnawed through a stem. 'You can punt with that,' he said. 'It will be quicker that way.'

Little Peter climbed cautiously on board. It was

rather scary because the clog wobbled, but the wooden deck felt sturdy.

'Smells of socks, eh?' said Tibby.

'Yes, yes,' said Little Peter who was not thinking about his nose. He grasped the reed pole and pushed off gingerly.

For the first time in the history of the Dwarfs of Nosegay, a dwarf was travelling by water – in an old farmer's clog.

There he went, round the high wire fence, with a hard push from the reed, and he stepped ashore in the land of Furtherup, where the willow trees stood.

'Hurrah!' cried Little Peter. 'I'm there!'

He had to go through a clump of stinging nettles and he went on his hands and knees, keeping as low as possible so that the leaves could not prick him.

'Tibby,' he called, as he crawled into view. 'Hallo, Tibby!' and he stretched his hand through the wire to the rabbit.

'Better pick some lettuce,' said Tibby.

Little Peter picked seven big lettuce leaves from seven lettuces and dragged them to the clog.

But potatoes were too heavy for a dwarf by himself. He could not even dig them up. There will have to be five of us, he thought, or ten, and the cart, that will do it.

'Are you coming back now?' called Tibby.

Little Peter didn't answer. He had ducked under the stinging nettles again and now he could feel something stroking his cheek – ouch? But it didn't sting, it tickled. It was not a leaf, it was a wing, the soft, bright wing of a butterfly.

'Daphne!'

Then Little Peter saw that the butterfly was pointing to something with her feelers. She was pointing underneath the stinging-nettle leaves, where there were rows of little balls: butterfly eggs.

'Daphne!' cried Little Peter again. 'Your children! That's where your caterpillar children will be. When will they come out?'

But the butterfly just stroked his dwarf cheek again and fluttered away.

'Hey, have you been stung?' called Tibby impatiently. 'Where have you got to?' But Little Peter could not tell him; he did not say a word the whole way home.

11 Freeing the Bees

Little Peter Nosegay was telling his story, his cheeks red with excitement.

'Ianto,' he said. 'Ianto, I sailed along, in the clog, across the water, round the wire fence to Furtherup. In the clog. We can fetch the potatoes in it. It's a big cargo boat, that clog. And we can – '

'How did you find the clog?' asked Tirian Nosegay.

'It was lying on the bank,' said Little Peter. 'It was lying in the grass. And Tibby pushed it in. Tibby, with his nose. Tibby said the clog smelled, smelled of socks.'

'Heavens,' cried Crooked Dirk.

'I dare not go on the water,' said Chick. 'Dwarfs don't sail. They belong on dry land.'

'Tcha!' cried Scutch Nosegay. 'Dwarfs don't belong in the air either, but we've been flying, in the bee basket.'

'That is so,' said Ianto the Eldest.

'Well,' said Crooked Dirk. 'If it's all true. You haven't even brought a carrot with you as evidence.'

Little Peter blushed. 'Just a bit of lettuce,' he said, 'For Tibby.'

'Yes, yes,' said Crooked Dirk. 'What good is that to us?'

Little Peter blushed still more brightly. He could have brought one little carrot with him, but he had not given it a thought, because Daphne had suddenly appeared from among the stinging nettles. Now he knew where her caterpillar children would come out of their eggs. And Little Peter didn't want to talk about that.

'Well,' he told Crooked Dirk, 'you'd better go and look. If you don't believe what I told you about the clog, go and see for yourself.'

Ianto Nosegay scratched his head 'Listen, Crooked Dirk,' he said. 'We –'

But none of the dwarfs was listening to Ianto. They could hear another sound: pounding rabbits' feet and an anxious rabbit voice: 'The bees! Help the bees!'

Eartwitcher came rushing through the tall heather, with Tibby and Scrabbletoes, like elephants in the jungle. 'The bees,' he panted. 'They can't get out. You'll have to help them, Dwarfs of Nosegay!'

'What has happened?' asked Ianto.

But the three rabbits had to get their breath back first.

'What a wind,' said Crooked Dirk. 'It feels like a storm.'

When the storm was over, Eartwitcher began: 'We were passing the hollow tree and there was buzzing inside.'

'Very loud,' said Tibby. 'And very bad-tempered.'

'Poor little bees,' cried Scrabbletoes. 'They're in pitch darkness, shut in.'

'How's that?' asked Ianto. 'There's a hole at the top, isn't there?'

'Yes,' said Eartwitcher, 'but the hole has been closed up.'

'With a nasty thing,' cried Scrabbletoes. 'A human thing. It was fluttering.'

Crooked Dirk sniffed. 'Stupid rabbit talk,' he said.

'Go and look,' said Tibby. 'There's something fluttering in front of the hole.'

'Must I always go and look?' cried Crooked Dirk.

'First at a clog and then at something fluttering. I shall be on the move all the time.'

But Little Peter had jumped onto Tibby's back.

'Come on!' he cried. 'Take us there, quickly. Off to the hollow pine!'

'Hey there,' cried Ianto, 'not so fast. Take axes and saws with you, and knives too.'

Ianto the Eldest organized everything.

Strong Scutch took the basket of tools and climbed on Eartwitcher's back. Little Peter, Tirian and Crooked Dirk climbed on Tibby's back and Scrabbletoes got Ianto and another two dwarfs. 'You do tickle!' squawked Scrabbletoes.

'Fusspot rabbit,' growled Crooked Dirk.

Off went the Dwarfs of Nosegay, dada-flop, dada-flop on bumpety furry backs through the heather. The rest followed on foot.

There really was something fluttering up there in the hollow tree. The entrance to the Bee City was completely closed.

'It's a sack,' said Ianto.

'You see!' squawked Scrabbletoes. 'Human beings!'

'Whoever did that is a fathead,' said Tirian. 'They must have done it to catch the bees – as if they would fly in there!'

The bees did not fly into the sack. The buzzed and zoomed and boomed furiously, down there in their city of smooth wax. You could hear them clearly.

'We've come to save you!' cried Little Peter. But could the bees hear him or understand him?

Scutch climbed up. 'There are nails in it!' he cried. 'The mouth of the sack is nailed to the tree all round the hole.'

Then the Dwarfs of Nosegay hauled the basket up to the top with much panting and sighing and began to chip and saw and cut and twist.

Sacking is tough and they had to go round the nails, all eighteen of them.

Scutch sawed the hardest.

'Soon the whole tree will be coming down,' said Crooked Dirk.

Little Peter chipped away, but from time to time he

also called to the bees to calm them down. 'It's us,' he called, *chip-chip*, 'we've come to let you out,' *chip-chip*. 'Come to let you out. Tell the queen. Tell Queen Zoe.'

If the bees did not understand them, he thought, they would attack the dwarfs as soon as they were free. Chick was so frightened by this idea that he stood trembling down below, wondering where to find a hiding-place.

Then Little Peter had an idea. 'Let's sing our song!' he cried. 'Our dwarf song. The bees know that.'

And so it was that ninety-nine little dwarfs sat side-by-side on a little branch of the hollow tree and sang their three-part song:

We are the dwarfs of the moor
And Nosegay is our name.
We live with the bees on the moor
And we're very glad they came.

As they sang they tugged at the sack, which was hanging by only two or three threads now, and pulled it off the last nail.

Zooomm! A cloud of bees billowed out like deep golden smoke and the dwarfs could see nothing more. But they could feel: tiny feet and feelers and heads. They sat there, quite overwhelmed by bees. Chick, down below, shrieked with terror.

But the bees were not stinging, they were kissing.

'Gracious me,' said Ianto, when the dwarfs were sitting round the fire in the hollow that evening. 'It's lucky bee kisses are dry, but a hundred is more than enough for me.' He wiped his cheeks once again

'That was their thank you,' said Little Peter.

12 *The Cargo Boat*

'There it is,' said Little Peter Nosegay. 'There.'

The dwarfs crowded together in the tall grass on the edge of the ditch. 'Let me, let me!' they cried, because they all wanted to look at once. And when they were all looking at once they took their caps off respectfully.

'He was right,' said Crooked Dirk. 'It really is a cargo boat.'

But the thing bobbing in the water, tied up with a piece of grass rope, was simply an old clog.

'We can get two potatoes in there easily,' said Scutch. 'Forward, lads, let's get sailing.'

They had brought the cart with them and spades to dig with. Ianto the Eldest told them what to do: 'Three dwarfs together in the boat,' he said. 'Little Peter mus punt to the land Furtherup with the reed pole and come back to fetch another three dwarfs.'

And that was what they did. Scutch, Tirian and Chick went first, Chick quaking with fear.

'Take spades with you,' said Ianto. 'And start digging a potato up right away.'

Little Peter thrust with his reed pole against the bottom of the ditch and the clog with the dwarfs on board moved like a real boat over the water. It rocked a little. 'Sit still!' cried Little Peter. He punted like a proper boatman; they sailed round the wire fence and soon afterwards the clog bumped against the bank of the land Furtherup where the potatoes and carrots grew.

'Watch out for the stinging nettles,' said Little Peter, when the dwarfs landed. Chick got his foot muddy, ugh, but at least he had not drowned.

So Little Peter travelled to and fro several times until there were enough dwarfs in the land Furtherup to do the work.

They needed seven potatoes for their winter supplies and a great many carrots. The finely-chopped carrots they had fetched a little time ago (thanks to the help of the bees) were no good any more. They had dried out and tasted horrible.

They dug, breathlessly, and nudged and shoved until a whole potato, as heavy as a full rain-butt, was above ground. Little Peter and Crooked Dirk rolled the potato to the clog, going carefully under the stinging nettles.

'What are you looking at?' Crooked Dirk asked from time to time. 'Are you frightened of getting stung?'

'Y-yes,' said Little Peter.

'I don't believe it,' said Crooked Dirk. 'You're looking for something.'

'Me?' said Little Peter. 'Not me!' But his wrinkled face was red, because he really was looking for something. Little Peter was looking for the eggs Daphne had shown him underneath the leaves of the nettles. But he could not see them anywhere now. Little Peter realized that the caterpillars had come out of their eggs – Daphne's children, who were also going to become butterflies.

'They've crawled away,' he muttered. 'How shall I ever find them again?'

'What's that you say?' asked Crooked Dirk.

'Oh, nothing,' said Little Peter.

They tipped the potato into the clog and went back to fetch the next one.

When there were two potatoes in the clog Little Peter punted back to the others, round the wire fence, and there the cargo was unloaded into the cart.

'One at a time,' said Ianto. 'We shall have to go to and fro with the cart seven times. To our hollow and back. And then a lot more times for the carrots.'

They had done the same thing before, for many days. But at that time there had been no wire fence.

'What we can't manage on the cart today,' said Ianto 'we'll hide in the ground here. Then we'll come back and fetch it tomorrow and the day after.'

'If only the rabbits keep away from it,' said one of the dwarfs.

'From the carrots, yes,' cried Little Peter. 'They're mad about carrots. You'll have to give them a few carrots, Ianto. They're hungry.'

'We shall see,' said Ianto.

Little Peter punted back in the cargo clog. Crooked Dirk was waiting for him. 'You should have been here,' he said. 'They're eating everything up.'

'What?' said Little Peter. 'The rabbits?'

'No, silly. They can't get in here. Caterpillars.'

Little Peter gave a shout. 'Where? Where, Dirk, where?'

'My, but you're nervy, lad. Are you scared of them?'

'Scared?' cried Little Peter. 'Those are the chil –'

But he didn't go on. He crawled to the place where Crooked Dirk was pointing. It was teeming with caterpillars, crawling over stems and leaves, fat caterpillars with lots of feet, and some of them with arched backs. 'Sweet little children!' cried Little Peter. 'Hello little –'

Crooked Dirk began to shout with laughter. 'Don't be so ridiculous, Peter. Those nasty creatures!'

'They're not nasty,' Little Peter called back. 'Not nasty.' He became very cross. 'They're going to be butterflies, just like – '

'Aha!' said Crooked Dirk. 'Aha, now I understand. Just like Daphne, you were going to say. Your great friend Daphne, the beautiful butterfly you are so in love with. Aha!' Crooked Dirk was a little bit mean.

'I'm not!' cried Little Peter. 'Daphne is married to Jacob and these are her children. I have to look after them, after her children.'

'Oh yes?' said Crooked Dirk. He laid a hand on Little Peter's shoulder. 'I'm only teasing,' he said. 'Let the caterpillars eat. Then they'll spin themselves into a chrysalis and next spring they will be butterflies all by themselves. You don't have to look after them.'

Next day the dwarfs went on digging up potatoes and carrots, rolling them to the clog and sailing them to the others. They hid everything in a hollow under the grass, and went back to their house in the moor with a single potato in the cart.

'I don't have to look after them,' thought Little Peter. But long ago Little Peter had found the chrysalis which Daphne had come out of and guarded it carefully. Should he – ? That might be a good idea.

Ianto was thinking: 'Will the rabbits keep away from the carrots?'

So the Dwarfs of Nosegay went home, not only with a potato in their cart, but with thoughts going round and round in their heads.

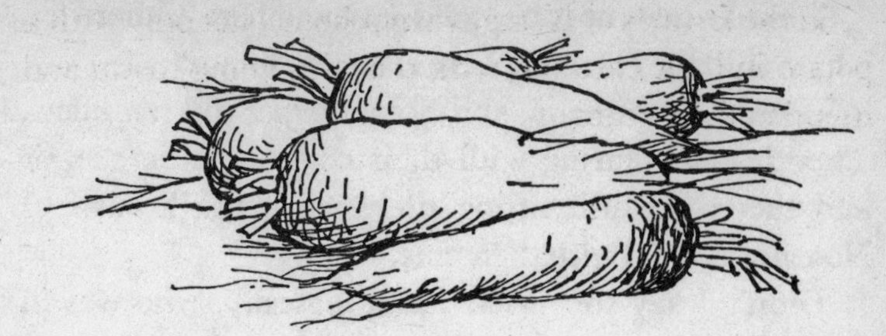

13 Carrots for the Rabbits and Something Else for Little Peter

Scrabbletoes, the nervous rabbit, came running into the burrow with an orange carrot in her mouth. 'Found it!' she cried. 'Just like that, in the grass. There's a whole lot of them.'

'Just like that?' asked Eartwitcher. 'That's dangerous.'

'Poisoned!' cried Tibby.

Scrabbletoes spat out the carrot and the other rabbits sniffed at it. 'Smells good, you know.'

They went to have a look by the bank of the ditch in the high grass, and it was true, there was a pile of carrots.

'Keep off!' cried Eartwitcher, for some of the rabbits were beginning to nibble. The carrots looked so delicious and they were so hungry. They sat in a circle round the store, staring at the carrots. Were they really poisonous?

'I think they must be,' said Eartwitcher. 'Otherwise, why would they be lying here all ready for us?'

Tibby did not know and Scrabbletoes did not know. They just sat staring with their cotton-tails in the air and they were still sitting there when the Dwarfs of Nosegay arrived with their cart.

'Didn't I say so?' cried Ianto Nosegay, who was in front. 'There won't be a carrot left, for sure.'

'There is, there is!' cried Little Peter. He had pushed his way bravely through the rabbits and was looking into the store. 'They're all there still – all but one. Dear rabbits, were you guarding them? Guarding our carrots instead of eating them? How kind!'

'Unbelievable,' said Tirian Nosegay.

Eartwitcher scratched his head. 'Er-hum . . . no. We thought, hum . . .'

'You thought: they belong to the dwarfs, so we won't touch them,' said Ianto. 'How extraordinarily kind. Then we'll help you and collect a whole mountain of carrots for you.'

Scrabbletoes began to giggle. 'Poisonous!' she squeaked. 'Teehee!' Tibby gave a hard nudge. 'Hold your tongue,' he hissed.

All the other rabbits held their tongues too. They helped the dwarfs to load the cart with carrots. They helped pull the cart to the dwarfs' winter store in the middle of the moor. And meanwhile Little Peter and ten little dwarfs were bringing more carrots from the land

Furtherup. To and fro along the ditch, sailing in the clog with a whole heap of orange carrots.

Little Peter thought this was fine, because it gave him a chance to look at Daphne's caterpillars. There were far fewer caterpillars than the time before, he could see. Had they crawled away? And if so, where? Or had they been eaten by birds?

At the end of the day, after the last crossing with the clog, Ianto said: 'Here you are, Eartwitcher. This pile of carrots is for you.'

Eartwitcher bowed his head. He did not dare to look at Ianto, but suddenly he said: 'Thank you very much, but it wasn't – I mean, we thought they were poisonous, so – '

Ianto began to laugh, showing a thousand wrinkles. 'I knew that,' he said, 'I could hear Scrabbletoes quite clearly. But I had planned all along to get you some carrots. As a punishment we'll come and live in your rabbit burrow in the winter. For three weeks, all hundred of us.'

'Oh,' cried the rabbits, 'oh good!'

On the way home to their hollow on the moor, Little Peter said: 'Ianto, I'm worried. Worried about the caterpillars.'

'Oh yes?' said Ianto. He knew that Little Peter wanted to look after them, because they were the children of Daphne and Jacob. 'You must stop worrying, lad.'

'Yes, but they're crawling away and hiding. Then they will spin themselves up and then they will come out again and I will never see them again. Never again.'

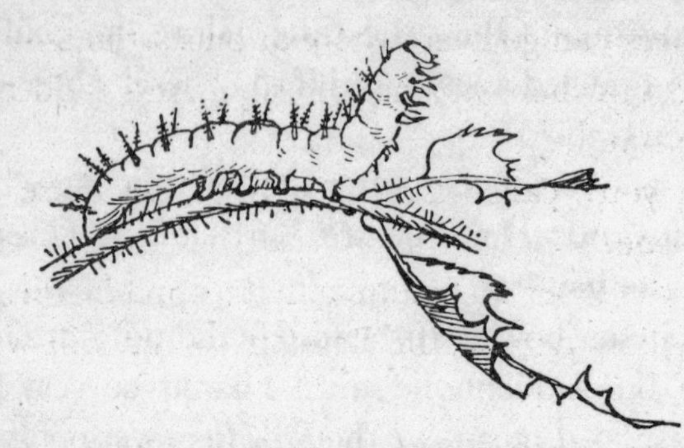

'You'll see them again in the Spring,' said Ianto. 'When they turn into butterflies.'

'But that's just what I want to see,' said Little Peter. 'I want to see it happening, just like Daphne.'

Ianto had no answer to that.

All the rest of the summer Little Peter went on fretting over the caterpillars. From time to time he sailed off in the clog to look under the stinging nettles in the land Furtherup. Fewer and fewer caterpillars were there, until, on his last trip, there was not a single one.

'You must collect honey,' said Crooked Dirk. 'You're always running off. You must join in and help.'

The moor was covered with purple flowers. The Dwarfs of Nosegay squeezed the honey from them, for their winter supplies as well, and the bees did the same.

There was a great buzzing and business. 'Hey bee, get off, that flower's mine,' someone would say now and then. But there were no real squabbles because the two races knew one another well now.

'The bees can go everywhere at once,' thought Little Peter. 'Everywhere at once. Easily.' And suddenly he began to run.

'Here, you!' called Crooked Dirk. 'Let those caterpillars alone!'

But Little Peter was running in the opposite direction, to the hollow tree, to the Bee City of smooth wax, to Queen Zoe.

'There now, Little Peter,' said Queen Zoe. 'I haven't seen you for a long time. How are the little Nosegays?'

'Oh, well,' said Little Peter. 'Very well. I wanted to ask you something. To ask for help.'

'Any time, little dwarf, any time,' said the Queen. 'You freed us when we were shut up. We will gladly do something in return.'

Little Peter told her his plan.

'You're a sly one,' said the Queen.

For the next few days Little Peter helped with the honey like a good lad.

'Not bothering about the caterpillar babies any more?' asked Dirk teasingly.

'No,' said Little Peter. 'They'll come to me themselves.'

'Haha!' said Crooked Dirk.

But when the heather stopped blooming and all the work was done Little Peter said: 'Today. I think they'll be coming today.'

'There's some smoke coming,' said Crooked Dirk, pointing to the sky.

Smoke?

It was a swarm of bees, buzzing as they flew. Hundreds of bees with threads hanging from their legs, and on the threads hung –

'Seven!' shouted Little Peter. 'You've found seven of them! How lovely!'

There were seven chrysalises, caterpillars in spun silk, Daphne's children who would become butterflies in the spring just as Daphne had done.

All the bee people had been looking for them, thousands of them looking among the stinging nettles: Here's one! Here's one! Buzzing to themselves; and the seven finest had been brought to Little Peter.

'Thank you!' called the dwarf. 'Thank you, just put them down here. I'll take good care of them all winter. Oh, and thank the Queen. Good, good.'

Crooked Dirk was staring open-mouthed. *All* the Dwarfs of Nosegay were staring open-mouthed, while the bees were already flying home. At last Ianto the Eldest said:

'Little Peter, we really ought to be calling you Big Peter.'

And Tirian Nosegay said: 'You think better than I do!'

And Scutch Nosegay said: 'I'm strong, but you're twice as bright.'

And Chick Nosegay said: 'How did you dare to ask them?'

'Haha,' laughed Crooked Dirk. 'Big Peter with seven butterfly children. You'll have to take them for walks in the spring to get the air, haha.'

They all laughed together and the peals of mirth of a hundred Dwarfs of Nosegay resounded over the big moor.

14 *A Dangerous Journey*

Little Peter had laid the seven chrysalises which the bees had brought him under his clump of heather. Neatly, side by side, with dry grass and leaves laid over them. So they were well hidden, because no one must be allowed to touch them.

'Haha,' said Crooked Dirk. 'Are you afraid of thieves?'

Little Peter turned red, but Ianto the Eldest said: 'Yes, thieves, the animal thieves of the moor. And frost. If it freezes, the chrysalises must be well protected.'

'Could they come in with us then?' asked Little Peter. 'Inside the mole-hill?' In the winter the Dwarfs of Nosegay lived deep underground in a mole tunnel.

'That's not necessary,' said Ianto the Eldest. 'All the same . . . perhaps they could after all. Bring them in if there's a hard frost. But don't forget to put them out again in the spring, otherwise the butterflies will come out in darkness.'

'Haha, butterflies in a mole tunnel!' laughed Crooked Dirk.

Little Peter nodded. 'I'll remember, Ianto,' he said, 'I'll remember for sure.'

The autumn was wet and cold and raw, with deep blue clouds from the north which shook white hailstones out over the moor.

'Do you know what?' said Ianto. 'We're going to the rabbits. We're going to spend a week in their fortress.'

'Fortress?' asked Little Peter.

'Yes,' said Ianto. 'A sort of castle. That's what the rabbits have underground. Passage-ways and halls, you'll see.'

'And carrots to eat,' cried Crooked Dirk.

That was what the dwarfs and rabbits had agreed on that day in the land Furtherup when they were collecting carrots in Little Peter's clog boat.

In the evening Ianto told the other dwarfs his plan. They sat shuddering with cold in their hollow, because their little fire did not burn well when the wood was wet. The smoke was making them cough.

'We're moving tomorrow morning,' he said.

'All hundred of us?' asked Tirian Nosegay.

'All hundred of us,' said Ianto. 'There's plenty of room in the rabbits' fort. And we'll take the cart with us, with tools and honey.'

'Why?' asked Scutch Nosegay.

'You never know,' said Ianto.

When it was light they loaded the cart: two saws, an

axe, lengths of rope, extra caps, a whole potato, the dwarf lamp, the big saucepan and of course the honey.

'Won't you be bringing the chrysalises?' Crooked Dirk asked Little Peter. 'Your dear little butterflies?'

'Stow that stuff,' cried Ianto. 'Come and help.'

A tin of bandages and ointment had to go in too. And acorns for bowling, because the dwarfs enjoyed that, and grass for making beds. The cart had never been so full before.

'Pull, lads, three at once, and push. One, two . . .'

'I've got a pain in my toes,' Chick whimpered.

'Stop grumbling!'

'Yes, but something is going to happen. When I get a pain in my toes something awful happens.' Chick was quaking with fear.

'It'll be the snow.'

'No, no, something much worse. Something black. I can see it, oh my little toe!' Chick's face turned quite white. Chick was always frightened.

'I'll protect you,' cried strong Scutch Nosegay.

But Tirian put his nose in the air. 'What rubbish,' he muttered. 'Push, men, forward!'

They were off.

Little Peter took one more look at his heather clump where the chrysalises were hidden. 'Goodbye, children,' he called, but not too loud because he didn't want Crooked Dirk to hear.

The rabbits lived under the pine trees. That was a long way off, right across the moor, past the land

Furtherup and a little bit further. The dwarfs made slow progress with their heavy cart.

Towards midday they made a halt for a snack.

'How's your toe feeling?' asked Ianto the Eldest.

'Worse and worse. It's pricking,' said Chick, casting a nervous glance at the sky.

'But there isn't a cloud to be seen,' said Ianto.

No, the sky was pure blue and that was lucky for the dwarfs, although the wind was cold.

'Show-off!' said Tirian Nosegay.

Later in the afternoon Tirian would not have said that.

He himself was the first to see what was coming: not cloud, not hail, not snow; no white terror, but a black one.

'Oh help!' cried Little Peter, who had seen it too. 'Oh help, crows!'

Flapping their wings and cawing raucously the black birds came rushing straight down on the dwarfs.

'You see, there it is!' screamed Chick Nosegay, diving under the cart.

Crows are dangerous to people as small as the Dwarfs of Nosegay. Crows catch mice and the dwarfs were scarcely any bigger.

'Get away!' yelled Ianto. 'Dive! Take cover!'

But where were they to hide? The heather was too thin to crawl under here and there was not a molehill in sight.

Shaking with fear, they stayed huddled round the cart.

'We must do something!' cried Tirian Nosegay, but he did nothing.

'Caw! Caw!' rasped the crows. They were already close by.

Then Scutch jumped up on to the cart, Scutch Nosegay, the bravest of them all. Grasping a saw, he flourished it in the air like a sword. 'We must fight!' he shouted, 'fight to the last man!' Brave he certainly was, but what can one dwarf saw do against a flock of crows?

'Just you wait!' shouted Scutch. He tipped some of the stuff out of the cart so that he could move better: the first-aid tin, the acorns and the big saucepan, which fell to the ground clattering with all the spoons inside it.

Aha, thought Little Peter. He noticed that the crows swung off to one side. Aha! Suddenly he crawled forward, turned the pan upside down on the heather and began to beat vigorously on it with two spoons. Clackety-clack.

'Come and help!' he called, 'come and help! All take a spoon and make a noise. They're afraid of noise, afraid of noise, crows are. Clackety-clack, and *shout*!'

It was just as if Little Peter had pronounced a magic spell. In three ticks there was a ring of dwarfs round the pan, each with two spoons, beating ding-ding on the copper bottom.

It rang out like a warning bell, together with the shouts and yells from a hundred throats (for Chick under the cart was yelling too) and there was also Scutch's lashing saw: suddenly the crows seemed to be swooping down on a dangerous band of savages.

It was enough to frighten anyone and the black flyers were frightened – they were suddenly scared stiff and swerved away, far from that terrible din. 'Krark!' they cawed hoarsely, vanishing across the moors.

'Just as I thought, they're cowards,' said Tirian Nosegay, sounding very doughty.

Crooked Dirk looked at him. 'Oh yes?' he said. 'But who was it who had the idea? Who began banging on the saucepan? Well?'

Tirian was silent.

It was Ianto the Eldest who answered: 'Little Peter, who should really be called Big Peter!'

'There, now!' cried Crooked Dirk.

Little Peter said nothing, but the rest of the way he walked beside Crooked Dirk, with his hand on his shoulder.

It was already growing dark when they reached the entrance to the rabbit burrow at last. 'Deary me,' sighed Scutch. 'I only hope they're in.'

Ianto stuck his head inside. 'Coo-ee!' he shouted. 'Here we are!'

'Who?' said a voice and there was Tib, his ears cocked with astonishment. 'Well, well, the Dwarfs of Nosegay! All hundred of you?'

'All hundred of us,' said Ianto the Eldest. 'And all hundred of us have come to stay.'

'Ahem,' said Tib. 'I mean, how jolly. Come inside.'

Crooked Dirk began to wriggle his nose in the air. 'I smell carrot soup,' he said.

And so the visit began.

15 *In the Burrow*

The rabbits' burrow was a place you could get lost in. Passages and side-passages and halls and bolt-holes and little rooms, all dug out of the hard yellow sand under the heather. There was not much light. Here and there a little daylight filtered through a crack in the ceiling; sometimes there was the green glow of a glow-worm and then of course the dwarf lamp which Ianto the Eldest was carrying.

'Don't go wandering about on your own,' said Ianto.

Tib and Scrabbletoes had to laugh at that. 'We'll teach you the way,' they said. 'Come on.'

The Dwarfs of Nosegay took each other by the hand, all hundred of them, and Ianto the Eldest held Tib fast by the tail. 'Here we go!'

They skipped along the passages in a long line, up,

down, round the bends, and behind them came Scrabble with her nose against Little Peter's back.

'This is the east passage,' said Tibby. 'And that's the south passage, and along here you come out under the dwarf pine and there's the escape way to the birch, and now we must go back.'

They turned about, all hundred dwarfs, and now it was Scrabble who was in front, with Little Peter at her tail.

'The north passage is here,' Scrabble began, 'and past the bend is the west – oh no, wait a minute, I mean to the left, but if you go straight on you get back to the great hall, but first we'll go right to the – '

'Not so fast,' cried Little Peter.

'ATCHOO!' sneezed Scrabble, terribly loudly. It echoed down the passageways and CHOO CHOO CHOO resounded from all sides, as if seven rabbits had sneezed.

'Hey, who's doing that-at-at?' came a voice from the distance. 'Where are you-ou-ou?'

It was Tib's voice.

'Here!' cried Little Peter. 'Ere-ere.'

More shouts came echoing back because the long line of dwarfs had broken in two. The thirty-eighth and thirty-ninth dwarfs, Crooked Dirk and Tirian Nosegay, had lost each other's hands in the darkness.

There were confused sounds of 'Oh oh oh, what now?'

'ATCHOO!' went Scrabble again.

'Come here, the other way!' called Tib.

'This way!' called Ianto Nosegay.

'Hold on!' cried Little Peter.

Tripping and stumbling, bumping and jostling, two processions of dwarfs were now moving down the burrow. One with Scrabble in front and thirty-eight little men behind, the other with Tib in front and sixty-two little men following each other.

'Hoo-hoo!' called the two rabbits, like trains, so that they did not bump into each other. But from time to time Scrabble went on with her ATCHOO and Little Peter could feel from the rabbit's tail that she was trembling.

'Are you ill?' asked Twitcher, when at last they were all sitting together in the great hall.

'I think I must be, a little,' said Scrabble. She went off to lie down in a corner, but Tib said: 'Go to your nest, my girl, that will be much better.'

Scrabble staggered into a passage, sneezing and with her long floppy ears flat across her back.

'Hm,' said Twitcher. 'We shall have to put off our carrot party until tomorrow.'

'That doesn't matter,' said Ianto. 'We shall get on very nicely here.'

'That's fine,' Tib cried cheerfully. 'You know your way around here now.'

The little dwarfs looked at each other. 'Well, er,' began Ianto warily, 'as to that . . .' and Crooked Dirk began to laugh. 'Ha ha, I got into a great muddle, north, south, up, left . . .' But Tirian Nosegay put his stubborn nose in the air: 'I know it perfectly,' he said.

'Oh yes?' said Chick, shivering, 'how clever of you, Tirian,' and that made Crooked Dirk laugh louder than ever. 'Off you go then, Knowall, and we'll see you back here in three days' time.'

But Tirian did not dare to go and they all laughed very loudly and from the seven passages the 'ha ha ha' came echoing back.

They played skittles with the acorns for a time until Scutch suddenly cried: 'I say, what's happened to Little Peter?'

Oh dear, Little Peter was nowhere to be found. 'Stupid dwarf,' said Tirian. 'He's obviously gone missing on the way.'

But that was not true. Crooked Dirk had only just seen him, here in the great hall. Crooked Dirk was suddenly very worried.

'Little Peter!' he called.

'Little Peter!' they all called. 'Where are you?' And the echo called back '– are you – are you – are you,' and then there was nothing. There was silence, an awful silence, an alarming silence. What could have happened?

'Let me go and look,' said Tib. 'I'll look with my nose.' Tib had a wonderful sense of smell.

Whiskers quivering, he began to sniff down the seven passage-ways, but it was not so easy because a hundred different dwarf smells were left there. 'What does he smell like?' asked the rabbit. 'I can't tell the difference between you very well with my nose.'

'Let's see,' said Ianto the Eldest, 'what does Little Peter smell like?'

'Well, of course,' said Dirk, 'he smells of Peter.'

They began shouting again, very loudly: 'Little P–' But they stopped at the P, because they heard an answer.

'Sssst!' it went.

And there was the little dwarf appearing from the sixth passageway, with a finger to his lips.

'Be quiet,' he whispered, 'Scrabble is very ill. Terribly, terribly ill.'

'What?' cried Tib.

'I've just been stroking her,' said Little Peter. 'Her nose is all blocked up and she's shaking and shuddering and she's hot, terribly hot.'

But Ianto asked: 'Have you been with her?'

Little Peter did not understand. 'Of course,' he said. 'How else could I know that . . .'

'Ha ha!' shouted Crooked Dirk. He was laughing even louder than before. He was laughing at Tirian Nosegay. 'You didn't dare go down the passage alone, eh? And no one dared, none of us knows the way, and who just goes? Little Peter!'

They all felt like cheering, but they didn't because of poor Scrabble.

'We must do something,' said Little Peter. 'Make her a drink, a horrible drink against the 'flu.'

Tib and Twitcher looked at each other. They had never heard of such a thing before. When a rabbit is ill it has to get better on its own, that has always been the rule. Get better, or die, there is nothing anyone can do about it.

'But we can,' said Ianto the Eldest. 'We can make the sick better. I shall examine Scrabble.'

Little Peter had to go ahead with the dwarf lamp, with Ianto and Tib behind him.

Poor Scrabble. She was lying on her side, trembling and panting. Ianto felt her paws, patted her back, stroked her whiskers and peeped under her eyelids. 'Hm,' he muttered, 'only 'flu, luckily. Myxomatosis would have been worse, because I don't know of any medicine for that.'

Tib knew what Ianto meant, although he didn't understand the long medical word. 'Do you have some medicine for 'flu?' he asked.

'Certainly,' said Ianto. 'Oak bark and water mint.'

'Water mint?' said Tib. 'That doesn't grow in the barren wintertime.'

'I know that,' said Ianto. 'But we have some dried leaves. We pick them in the spring and keep them.'

'Wonderful,' said Tib. 'We'll go and gnaw some bark from the trees.'

They did, but when Ianto opened the tin of bandages and ointments he could see there was something missing. The Dwarfs of Nosegay had forgotten to bring their water mint leaves with them.

'How silly,' said Tirian.

But Little Peter said: 'I'll go and fetch them, on Tib's back, tomorrow morning.' He was thinking: I can go and have a look at my cocoons at the same time, at my butterfly babies.

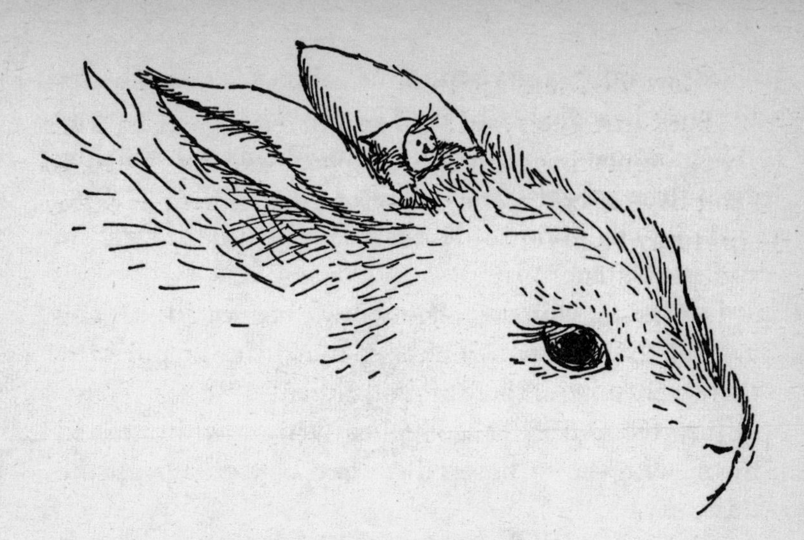

16 A Bitter Drink for Scrabble

It was cold. There was white hoar-frost on all the branches, on every pine needle, on every blade of grass, and the moor looked like a linen sheet.

'Brrrr,' said Tib.

'Ooooh,' said Little Peter.

They had got up early in order to be back as quickly as possible with the water mint leaves they were going to fetch for poor sick Scrabble.

Little Peter climbed on to Tib's back. 'Not too fast now,' he said. 'I shall catch cold too, if you go too fast.'

Tib ran quite slowly for a little way, then faster and then faster still. His back joggled like a horse's and Little Peter had to cling on tight to the ears. He leaned forward, with his nose right in the rabbit's fur. 'It's better like this,' he called. 'Go fast, Tib, very fast.'

Tib rushed ahead with hops and bounds so that the dwarf rose and fell like a real rider.

'I'm flying,' said Little Peter. 'I'm flying through the endless whiteness.'

He was not thinking about crows, nor were there any around. He was not thinking about foxes or polecats; there were none of those around either.

Just Tib and Peter, galloping over the white frosted moor, with the early sun like a red balloon against the misty sky.

'Right a bit,' called Little Peter. He had just looked up and he knew the way perfectly.

The mole-hill where the Dwarfs of Nosegay kept their stores was white too, as if someone had been sprinkling caster sugar over it.

Little Peter crawled inside and appeared a moment later with the dried mint leaves. 'Smell good, don't they,' he called.

But Tib's nose was in the air. 'I smell frost,' he said.

'It certainly is cold,' said Little Peter. 'Bitter, biting cold.'

'I know,' said Tib, 'but I mean hard frost. And icy wind.'

'Oh, let's get back at once then, at once – no! Wait! Stop!'

Tib flapped his ears. 'What's up with you?'

'My cocoons!'

'Your what?'

'Cocoons,' cried Little Peter. 'My little butterflies, my wrapped-up caterpillars I mean, the butterfly children I mean, I must rescue them.'

'Rescue?'

'From the frost,' cried Little Peter.

He ran to his clump of heather and began to scrabble

among the dried-up leaves with his bare hands. It was cold, icy cold.

'What are you doing now?' asked Tib.

Little Peter said nothing. One by one, very cautiously he pulled out the cocoons and dragged them with numb fingers to the mole-hill. 'They must go inside,' he explained. 'They must go underground because of the frost. That's what Ianto said, Ianto the Eldest said that.'

'Will butterflies come out of those?' asked Tib, because rabbits don't know that kind of thing.

'Won't they just!' said Little Peter. 'Lovely ones. Daphne's children, and Jacob's. In the spring. Lovely ones.'

He sealed up the mole-hill and at the same speed as before they went back to the burrow, Little Peter keeping his hands warm in the furry ears.

'Cold!' yelled Tib. But it didn't last long.

All the other Nosegay dwarfs had only just woken up when Tib and Peter rushed in.

'That's nice,' said Ianto the Eldest.

They powdered the oak bark, which the rabbits had nibbled off a tree the night before. They chopped up the mint leaves and stirred them in water for poor sick Scrabble. But she thought the drink was disgusting.

'Ugh, bitter!' she moaned.

'Drink it up,' ordered Ianto.

'Bitter as gall,' groaned Scrabble.

'Drink it down,' ordered Tib.

'Bitter as . . . as . . . baaah!' Scrabble complained.

'Swallow it down,' ordered Twitcher.

'Yes, but . . .'

'Stop whining!' cried Ianto, Tib and Twitcher

together, and Little Peter said: 'It will make you better, Scrabble. Quite, quite better.'

'Achoo!' she sneezed.

'That's good luck,' growled Ianto.

Scrabble took a gulp and another gulp and swallowed; her rabbit's face looked like a witch's mask, the taste was so horrible.

She was given a mouthful of honey by Ianto and after that she went to sleep, her rabbit's face like an angel's.

It did help. The 'flu vanished from her body and next day Scrabble was hopping through the burrow again as if nothing had happened. Hurrah for the dwarfs.

They held the carrot party the same evening, all together in the big hall, with a very small fire which the dwarfs had laid in a corner under a crack in the roof for the smoke to go out. The rabbits had never seen anything so nice before.

They ate carrot soup out of the big saucepan.

They ate chopped carrots with honey.

They ate carrot pudding with blackberry sauce.

They drank carrot juice with redcurrants.

'Oof,' said Crooked Dirk, 'what a carry-on with carrots.'

Everybody had to laugh, including the rabbits, and after laughter came singing, which only the dwarfs could do, and Scutch beat time with a spoon on the empty saucepan. They sang about the crows:

> 'The crows, the crows they scatter
> from biff, bop and bang:

the clatter, the clatter
of spoons on a pan!'

'Pang!' cried Crooked Dirk, 'otherwise it won't rhyme.'

'Oh, you, what does it matter?'

'A song must rhyme,' Crooked Dirk insisted. 'Bang and pan won't do. Either the *pan* goes *ban*, or the *pang* goes *bang*.'

'Yes, yes,' said Ianto the Eldest.

Tirian Nosegay sniffed.

'The spoon goes *pang*,' cried Little Peter.

'Pang, pang!' shouted the dwarfs and the rabbits stopped their ears.

'Quiet!' called Ianto. 'Quiet!'

Ianto the Eldest got up and went to the fire in the corner. He sat down sedately beside it and said: 'Now, Dwarfs of Nosegay, rabbit friends, I am going to tell you a story. The story of Virgil Nosegay and the Broom Giant.'

'Yes!' they cried. 'Yes, yes!'

They sat down close to him, quiet as mice.

Little Peter leaned against Crooked Dirk in case it was a little bit spooky . . .

17 The Story of Virgil Nosegay

'Virgil Nosegay' – Ianto began –'was the hundred and first of us, a fat dwarf with a round head full of silly ideas. Everyone said: 'Virgil is brave!' But that was only because he was too silly ever to see danger. He jumped into deep holes – and we had to haul him out again. He climbed high trees – and we had to lower him down on ropes. He laughed at crows – and we had to pull him quickly behind the bush.

' "Lads," said Virgil one day, "I have heard that there is a giant who is a hundred and one times as big as we are. I want to see that, so I'm going. Good-bye."

' "Hey," we cried, "Virgil, do not do it!"

' "Not?" he asked. "Why not?"

' "Because we're not going with you and we shan't be able to rescue you."

' "Rescue me?" asked Virgil. "What do you mean?"

' "Because," we all shouted together, "the giant will catch you and put you in a bird cage, in a mouse trap, in a jar, under a flower pot; because the giant will fatten you up, mince you small, turn you into sausages, fry you in the frying pan, eat you up, swallow you down; the giant will – "

' "Fine!" cried Virgil. "Those really will be adventures. Good-bye!"

'He went, and we watched him go with tears in our eyes, because we liked him. But perhaps he would fall in a hole on the way and we would be able to rescue him again. We hoped he would, but Virgil did not fall down a hole or climb a high tree or laugh at crows and in four days he reached the giant's house, wet through, because it had been raining.

' "Giant!" called Virgil. "Are you there?"

'But the giant was not at home. Virgil crept under the door to see the house from the inside: the tiles in the passage, the tiles in the kitchen, the pans and forks and the copper tap, the sofa in the living-room, the slippers under the bed, the waste-paper basket and the carpet, as high as a cornfield.

' "Yes," he muttered, "everything is certainly bigger here, but is it a hundred and one times bigger?"

'He wanted to measure it all, but suddenly the front door opened and a voice thundered: "Who's been making these muddy footprints?"

' "I have!" Virgil called back.

'The giant walked down the passage, over the passage tiles and over the kitchen tiles, along the sofa, along the bed, past the waste-paper basket and on to the rug. "Muddy marks everywhere!" he cried.

'And where they stopped stood Virgil.

' "What a whopper you are," said the dwarf. "I'm glad to have seen you."

' "You nasty little dirty mark-maker!" shouted the giant, stooping to pick Virgil up. But Virgil said:

' "You're a nasty big mark-maker yourself. Take a look at your own muddy footprints!"

'The giant saw his big black footprints on the rug, by the waste-paper basket, by the bed, by the sofa and on the tiles.

' "Sweep it up!" he bellowed. "Take the broom, you bit of a shrimp, and sweep it all up."

' "Oh, very well," said Virgil.

'He went to the kitchen, broke off a few twigs from the giant's broom and began to sweep up the muddy footprints off the tiles in the passage; his own little ones and the giant's enormous ones.

'Just a minute, he thought, I can measure these. One sole of the giant's foot should be the same length as a hundred and one of my shoes.

'He placed one shoe on one of the giant's muddy footprints and took neat little steps, heel to toe, heel to toe, four, five, six, seven, eight . . .

' "What are you doing out there?" the giant shouted from the living-room.

' "Keep quiet," said Virgil, ". . . nine, ten eleven, twelve . . ."

' "Sweep!" shouted the giant.

' "Yes, yes," said Virgil, measuring eagerly, ". . .

thirty-one, thirty-two, thirty – . It's wrong! It doesn't even add up to thirty-three! You're nothing like a hundred and one times as big as I am, only thirty-three times!"

' "What's that you say?"

' "Thirty-two and a half times!" cried Virgil.

'The giant came to look. "Haven't you finished yet?"

' "No," said Virgil. "You've disappointed me. I thought you were bigger."

' "Big enough to squeeze you up," shouted the giant.

' "Of course," said Virgil, "I can see that. But they said a hundred and one and it's only thirty-two and a half. I must go and tell them at once. Good-bye!"

' "Hey!" shouted the giant as Virgil walked to the front door. "Here, you! Sweep first, then I'll put you under a flower pot."

' "Oh yes," said Virgil, "they told me that. Under a flower pot, or in a jar, or in a mouse trap. But that won't be true either. Good-bye now."

' "*Come here!*" bellowed the giant. "You're going into the frying pan."

' "Rubbish," said Virgil. "Just like the sausage and the eating up and swallowing down. They've made a fool of me with their hundred and one. Sweep it yourself".

'The giant put his foot against the door and grabbed at the little dwarf with his thick fingers.

' "Wash your hands before eating!" shouted Virgil. "They're jet black, phoo, where have you been?"

'There was enough room next to the thirty-two and a half size giant foot to slip under the door. Virgil did so. "If you had been a hundred and one times me, giant, I would have stayed!" he called. "Good-bye!"

'When the giant jerked the door open Virgil was nowhere to be seen. There were not even any footprints in the wet sand and the giant had to sweep up the rest of the muddy footprints himself.

' "And he's still sweeping," said Virgil when he came back to us after a four-day walk. "He's sweeping and sweeping. In fury, because I said he was so small . . ." '

18 *Storm, Return, and What the Storm Had Done*

'Did that really happen?' asked Little Peter. 'Is it really true about the giant, Ianto?'

All through the story the Dwarfs of Nosegay had shivered and laughed at the same time. The rabbits had done the same, but they looked a little disbelieving.

'Virgil told me the story himself,' said Ianto.

'Made it up, you mean,' said Crooked Dirk. 'No one could lie as well as Virgil.'

'Is he really true then?' asked Little Peter. 'Is Virgil true? I never heard of him before. Never.'

'You were too small, Little Peter,' said Tirian. 'He's been gone a long time.'

'Where did he go?'

'Well . . .' Ianto's old face wrinkled up. 'Adventuring.'

Little Peter thought about it all for a long time, about the adventure, and did not pay much attention to Tibby, Scrabble and Twitcher, who were dancing a rabbit dance. The awkward creatures didn't look all that attractive anyway; they were rather like a pack of elephants. But the dwarfs clapped loudly when they had finished and said they thought the dance was wonderful.

'Almost on my toes,' grumbled Crooked Dirk. 'I don't call that dancing.'

Scutch prodded him in the back. 'Ssshh!' he whispered. 'Don't be so rude.'

Then the dwarfs played another game of skittles with the acorns and the rabbits tried to play too, but they were too big and were quite unable to throw with their paws.

That was the end of the carrot party. Everyone went off to sleep and the rabbit burrow became silent. But in the middle of the night there was a racket from outside. Howling, roaring and reverberating, as if someone were shouting very loudly down the passage or as if the echo were sounding all by itself.

'What's that?' The dwarfs were startled into wakefulness.

'I say, Tib, do you hear that?' cried Tirian. 'Have the moor witches broken out?'

Little Peter began to tremble and his teeth chattered.

'Are you frightened?' asked Crooked Dirk.

'N-no, c-cold,' shuddered Little Peter.

All the dwarfs could feel it: an ice-cold draught was blowing in gusts through the room.

'Tibby! Scrabble!' called Ianto.

The rabbits woke up. 'Oh,' they said, yawning. 'A storm outside.'

As if there were nothing special about it.

But the storm became a hurricane, howling and roaring, and it grew steadily colder, as if the wind were blowing down over the moor straight from the North Pole.

It didn't worry the rabbits in their thick furry coats, but the dwarfs crept close together and no one shut an eye again all night.

Tib said it was coming, thought Little Peter. Lucky I put my cocoons safely in the mole-hill.

The storm went on next day and the temperature was twenty below freezing. The rabbits were still able to go outside to collect dry twigs for the dwarfs to make a fire. They sat huddled round it, coughing in the smoke which the wind blew back again through the crack in the roof.

'What a smell,' said Scrabble.

'Yes,' said Tibby. 'But the little fellows have no fur and they would freeze without it.'

The storm lasted two more days but it died down at last and the dwarfs got up.

'We're going,' said Ianto the Eldest. 'We're going home again, to our mole-hill. It was very jolly with you and thank you very much for having us.'

They loaded up the cart.

'Thank you, thank you, thank you,' said the little

dwarfs. A hundred thank you's rang throught the rabbit burrow and the echo shouted back *you-you-you* a hundred times more.

'Good-bye!' said their three rabbit friends. 'Run quickly, before the snow comes.'

'Can you smell it?' Little Peter asked Tib.

'Well, no,' said Tibby. 'Not yet.'

'Good-bye then!'

It was still very cold, but the dwarfs warmed up as they walked. Their cart rattled along the path, luckily no longer as full as on their first trip because they had eaten a great many of their stores.

The big saucepan was on top in case the crows came.

'We start beating it with the spoons at once,' cried Scutch.

But no crows came. A great tit came.

'Hallo, Nosegays!' cried the great tit. 'Where have you been, you Dwarfs of Nosegay?'

'With the rabbits,' said Ianto the Eldest.

'I've been looking for you everywhere,' cried the great tit. 'The bee tree has split.'

'What?' cried Little Peter. 'What did you say?'

'The pine tree where the bees have their city was split in the storm. There's a great crack in it.'

'What about the bees?' asked Ianto.

'They're still there. The city wasn't touched, but it's cold.'

'Oh!' cried Little Peter. 'We must go there. Quick, Ianto, we must go to the bees.'

'But what can we do for them?' asked Tirian. With all his cleverness, Tirian Nosegay could not think of anything.

But Crooked Dirk said: 'Let Little Peter go and I'll go with him. Who else is coming?'

Twenty-one dwarfs put up their hands. They took the cart with them in case they needed tools. The rest followed Ianto and they took the dwarf lamp with them because they needed light in the mole-hill.

'Get back before dark now!' called Ianto.

The great tit flew ahead of Little Peter and his group of dwarfs, heading for the gnarled pine tree, to save the bees' city.

But how?

19 *Freezing Cold in Bee City*

When Little Peter and his twenty-one dwarfs reached the gnarled pine tree they saw that it was standing all askew. The storm had almost overturned it and there was a great crack in the trunk. You could look right into the hollow in the tree and see the honey-comb houses of Bee City inside.

'Cold!' cried Little Peter. 'How cold they must be, those bees.'

'I hope they haven't frozen to death,' said Crooked Dirk.

'Oh no! No, no!' Little Peter turned pale, but he was brave enough to climb in; he could just squeeze through the crack.

'Bees!' he shouted. 'Queen Zoe!'

There was no one to be seen. Little Peter ran across the bee square and through the gate to the palace. The slippery wax corridor felt icy cold, but further up the cold seemed to grow less and suddenly Little Peter thought he heard a feeble buzzing from somewhere in the depths.

'Queen Zoe!' he shouted again.

'Who's there?' came a faint reply.

'It's me!' called Little Peter.

One narrow passageway led downwards and the little dwarf allowed himself to slide down it. He landed in the palace cellars and there sat the Queen, surrounded by bees. The cellar was packed with them.

'Ah, Little Peter,' she said. 'Is it you?'

'Yes, Your Majesty, yes, how terrible, I mean how wonderful that you're still alive, and your people. Are you cold?'

'We're all cold,' said Queen Zoe, shivering. 'Very c-cold.'

'We'll have to cover it up,' said Little Peter. 'Cover up the crack I mean, stop it up.'

'Zoomm,' cried the bees, and that meant: 'How?'

'Oh, how?' said Little Peter. 'Yes, how, I don't know. I –'

But the Queen interrupted him. 'When Little Peter says something, he does it,' she said. 'You keep going, Little Peter. You can do things without knowing how.'

Little Peter turned rather pink. 'Thank you,' he said, and clambered up again, slipping and sliding.

'They're still alive, they're still alive, quick!' he called to the other dwarfs.

But how were they to close the crack?

They tried sand but it was frozen too hard, and too grainy.

They tried twigs of heather, but the wind could blow through them.

They tried dried leaves and pine needles but they wouldn't stay in place.

'If only we had three hundred caps and shawls, they would do,' said Crooked Dirk.

But they hadn't.

Right, thought Little Peter, if only we had some rags ... He walked thoughtfully round the tree, as if expecting a rag to fall from the air, and a rag was exactly what he found, for there, lying there still, was the big piece of jute, the jute sack which the dwarfs had torn away from the tree in the summertime when it had been nailed over the entrance to catch the bees.

There was the same jute sack, lying at his feet.

'Here!' shouted Little Peter. 'Here, I've found something!'

It was a great business getting the sack loose, because it was frozen hard to the ground. The dwarfs hacked away with their axe, heaved with the shovel and tugged with their hands until Crooked Dirk said: 'Blow!' Then they crouched down and blew their warm breath on to the jute sack to thaw the frost.

It was late afternoon when they got the thing loose

and it was already dusk when they started work on the leaning tree trunk. They had rolled the sack up like a sausage, and pushing and shoving and prodding, they forced it into the crack. At last it sat tight; there was not a peep-hole to be seen. Frost and wind could no longer reach the bees.

Tired out and with numb fingers, the dwarfs slid down again. 'That's done!' they puffed. 'Thanks to Little Peter.'

'Yes, yes,' said Crooked Dirk. 'That's true. But now it's almost dark and it will soon be pitch dark. How are we to get home?'

They were shivering. The moor lay before them, dark and cold. If they were to lose their way . . .

'We could climb inside the hollow tree,' suggested one.

'Really! We can't get twenty-one of us in there,' said Crooked Dirk.

It was growing rapidly darker.

'We should have taken the lamp,' said Little Peter, 'the lamp.'

And it almost seemed as if he had spoken a magic spell, because there, in the distance, was a little light coming towards them.

'Hey there!' someone yelled.

It was Tirian Nosegay, coming to look for them with the dwarf lamp.

'I wanted to do something,' he said. 'After all that thinking, I wanted to *do* something.'

'What a good thing,' said Crooked Dirk.

And with the lamp before them, the dwarfs walked back in a long line to the mole-hill. Over the cold and gloomy moor they walked, thinking about the bees' city which they had saved. Deep beneath the mole-hill, where it was warm and cosy, the big pan was bubbling on the fire, full of delicious soup.

20 *Daphne's Children*

On the first sunny day in March the Dwarfs of Nosegay appeared from their mole-hill. They stretched themselves and yawned with wide-open mouths, they swung their arms and began to rush round, yelling like madmen.

'The spring, the spring, hurrah for the spring!'

'Don't start cheering too soon,' said Crooked Dirk.

'Oh, you,' cried Scutch Nosegay. He was swinging from a branch of heather to exercise his strong arms. 'Oh, you, just feel the warm sunshine and the balmy wind!'

Ianto the Eldest said: 'Perhaps the cowslips are out already. Who's coming to look in the meadow?'

'It's still too early,' said Tirian.

But they went to the meadow all the same, past the hedge at the end of the moor, in order to have a nice walk and generally nose around. Even Chick went with them because Chick was mad about flowers. 'There are always daisies,' he said.

Only Little Peter stayed at home, because he was busy with his cocoons. One by one he pulled them out of the mole-hill and hung them up carefully by their own thread. They hung side by side on his clump of heather, but well hidden, so that no crows or other birds or beasts would spot them.

What a good thing, he thought, that I took them inside before the frost began. I wonder if all seven will come out!

He lay down comfortably in the sun to watch them and tried to think of names for the butterfly children.

Jorinda and Beatrice and Angelica and Grizelda – but there would be boys too, of course, so they would be William and Bernard and Alexander and . . . Virgil! But how many girls and how many boys would come from seven cocoons? Four and three? Or one and six?

Little Peter was still thinking it over when the other dwarfs came back from the meadow. The cowslips were still in bud, they told him, but Chick had found three daisies.

The weather stayed fine and next day a buzzing swarm of bees flew over with a message from Queen Zoe. Could Little Peter come to the hollow tree with a couple of dwarfs and the cart?

'Go right away,' said Ianto. 'I think the Queen wants to thank you.'

He was right.

The gnarled pine tree was still standing askew and the jute sack was still packed tightly into the crack. Little Peter climbed up to the entrance at the top and let himself drop inside. The bee city was full of life; the bees were ready to start their flights again and even Queen Zoe had come out of her palace. She was lying on her litter by the entrance and she beckoned Little Peter to her.

'For the second time,' she said gravely, 'you, the Dwarfs of Nosegay, have saved our bee people. To thank you I have a very special present for you. Here you are.'

Two bees pulled a cloth aside and there stood a chest, a gleaming chest made of white wax, decorated with squirls and pictures of flowers and bees. 'FOR THE DWARFS OF NOSEGAY,' was written on it in large capital letters. 'You can use that as a treasure chest,' said Queen Zoe. 'But before that you will have to' – she laughed – 'lick the honey out of it.'

The two bees threw back the lid and Little Peter saw that the chest was filled to the brim with delicious honey.

'Oh!' he cried. 'Thank you, Queen. Thank you, Zoe, er Queen Zoe, thank you very much!'

With the help of four more dwarfs he shoved the chest upwards and out through the hole, lowered it down the trunk and loaded it on the cart.

What a feast there was when he came back with it! 'That will last a very long time,' said Ianto.

At evening in their den by the crackling fire the dwarfs each had a mouthful, eating with a spoon from the opened chest.

'The sooner we finish it,' said Tirian, 'the sooner we will be able to keep our treasures in it.'

'Have we got all that many treasures?' said Crooked Dirk.

'We'll go and look for some,' cried Scutch. 'We'll look for treasure. Gold and silver and precious stones. Dwarfs are supposed to have those.'

'Calm down,' said Ianto the Eldest. 'We're not ordinary dwarfs. We're the Dwarfs of Nosegay.'

'What do you mean, Ianto?'

'I mean that we only go looking for what we need and what we don't need we leave. Unless it comes of its own accord.'

'Oh,' said Little Peter in a low voice.

Three weeks later the treasure chest was empty. One early April morning Little Peter was leaning right over it to lick the last trace of honey from the bottom when Crooked Dirk came by and gave him a slap on the behind.

'Hey, stop that!' cried Peter crossly.

'Your cocoons,' said Crooked Dirk. 'I came to warn you that your cocoons are coming out.'

Little Peter had never run so fast before. In three shakes he was under his clump of heather, and there they hung: six butterflies, hanging by their feet, their wings unfolding slowly.

'Jorinda!' he cried. 'Angelica, Beatrice, William, Grizelda . . . er, er . . .!' Little Peter had forgotten the other names in his excitement, and he did not yet know who was who, when six brilliant butterflies fluttered into the air in a cloud of red and black and white.

Six butterflies.

The seventh cocoon was still hanging from the branch of heather. Would the last child of Daphne and Jacob not be coming out? Little Peter could not believe it.

21 *The Last Butterfly and Someone Else*

Little Peter stayed up all night by the seventh cocoon. He lay on his back gazing at the stars. The Great Bear right above his head gave seven winks; the dwarf Rider on the second star of the Bear switched on and off; great Arcturus climbed up out of the east and the heavenly Twins sank in the west. Later in the night the moon came out as well, like a half-eaten slice of melon.

How slowly the time passes, thought Little Peter, so slowly, when you're lying watching.

In the morning Crooked Dirk came to him. 'You're being foolish, Little Peter,' he said. 'Go to sleep now, I'll keep watch for you.'

'Truly?' asked Little Peter. 'Will you truly do that?'

Crooked Dirk nodded. He watched all day beside the cocoon and Little Peter watched again the following night. For three days and three nights they watched in turn.

'It won't be coming out now,' said Crooked Dirk.

Ianto the Eldest agreed with him.

'Throw it away,' said Tirian Nosegay.

'I think that's sad,' cried Chick.

'Perhaps we ought to break it open,' suggested Scutch, 'then we could see it.'

'No!' shouted Little Peter. He was very unhappy. And he was still more unhappy when the dwarfs decided they would all go to the meadow to celebrate the spring.

'The clover is out,' said Ianto. 'Pink and white, and the dandelions and the blue speedwell. We're going to get honey and we'll be there all day.'

Little Peter did not watch that night. His eyes closed of themselves and he dreamed a strange dream. The cocoon opened, but no butterfly appeared; something else appeared, a grinning dwarf face, and everyone was glad. There were shouts, but Little Peter could not understand what they were saying.

He woke up with a start.

'Are you coming?' came a shout.

The dwarfs were ready, carrying their pots to be filled with honey.

Little Peter shook his head.

'As you like,' said Ianto and off they went, singing, in a long line across the moor, to greet the spring. The sun was shining in the blue sky, the wind carried the sweet scent of cows and all nature was merry.

Little Peter looked after them with tears in his eyes. Then he looked at the cocoon, which hung silent and motionless on the twig.

What can I do, he wondered, what can I do? I can't leave it all alone but I want to go with the others, I want to go too ... Suddenly he thought: why shouldn't my cocoon go too, why shouldn't it come to the spring festival with me?'

'What a wonderful idea!' cried Little Peter. 'Then I can do both!'

No sooner were the words out than he took the cocoon in his·arms, cut it loose from the heather and rushed after the others with it.

'They'll laugh at me,' he thought, 'But that won't worry me. Not a bit.'

He overtook them, panting, and joined the line.

'Ha ha!' laughed Scutch.

'You're nuts,' said Tirian.

'Funny Little Peter,' laughed the others.

But one of them did not laugh: Crooked Dirk. He

said: 'I'll carry it for you, Little Peter, as soon as you're tired.'

And so he did. Crooked Dirk, the tease, carried the cocoon for the last stretch before they reached the meadow.

There Little Peter hung the cocoon up on a tall sorrel, dancing in the wind, so that he could keep an eye on it while he and the others looked for honey in the meadow flowers. All the dwarfs could keep an eye on it, and so could the bees, and the rabbits which sat nibbling the tender grass.

It was the bees who came to warn Little Peter some time later. Buzzing round his head and buzzing round the cocoon, they called him over.

'He's coming out!' shrieked Little Peter excitedly. 'My last butterfly child is coming out!' He said nothing more, but he knew that the bees knew.

Ianto called all hundred dwarfs together in a big ring to sit round the sorrel.

Tib, Scrabble and Twitch sat side by side behind them and a thousand bees hovered in a buzzing cloud above them.

So the butterfly came out, the seventh child of Daphne and Jacob and the most beautiful of them all. While its wings spread slowly the other six came fluttering past and to the loud rejoicing of dwarfs, rabbits and bees, he lifted himself into the air.

'There you are,' said Crooked Dirk. 'You were right after all, Little Peter. Now what's his name?'

And Little Peter, without stopping to think for a moment cried:

'Virgil!'

'Virgil!' cried all the dwarfs together. 'Hello, Virgil, so you've come at last?'

Butterflies cannot talk.

So who was it who answered? The answer did not come from the sky, it came from the grass.

Scutch Nosegay looked round; Chick, Tirian, Crooked Dirk and all the others, the rabbits, the bees and finally Little Peter looked round. All of them looked towards a thick clump of grass behind which something was moving. A grinning face appeared, a sturdy arm, a fat tummy, a –

'Virgil!' yelled Ianto the Eldest.

'Virgil!!' yelled the rest.

The hundred and first Dwarf of Nosegay had returned.

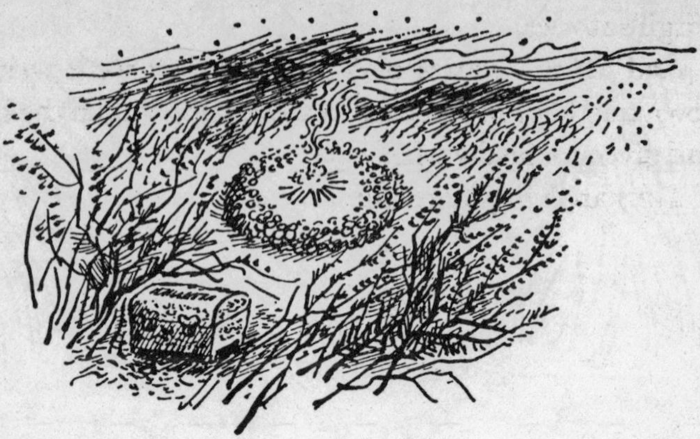

'What a reception!' he said. 'How did you know I was coming?'

'Ahem,' said Ianto, 'hem, well, we didn't know, or perhaps . . .'

'I dreamed it!' cried Little Peter.

'Good gracious,' said Virgil, 'if it's not Little Peter! What a clever little chap you've grown up to be.'

'He's called Big Peter now,' said Ianto the Eldest.

'Yes,' said Crooked Dirk, 'because he can stand up to teasing.'

They held a tremendous party, with the bees and the rabbits, and it lasted until evening.

That night, under the winking stars, a hundred and one Dwarfs of Nosegay sat round their crackling fire in the hollow, in the middle of the moor, and listened to Virgil's stories.

And all the stories of Virgil Nosegay were written down and kept in the wax treasure chest which the bees had given to the dwarfs.

They are lying there still.

Hello, I'm SMUDGE. I love books!
YOUNG PUFFIN
Sometimes I like listening to stories...
READ ALOUD
READ ALONE
... sometimes I like an easy short story that I can read on my own...
STORY BOOK
...and sometimes I settle down with a big story book - with lots of nice pictures.
You'll find me on the cover of every
YOUNG PUFFIN.
Pick me up and you'll love my books!